PRETEND

A Blackcreek Novel

By: Riley Hart

Published by

Riley Hart

The characters and events portrayed in this book are fictitious. Any similarity to real persons, living or dead is coincidental and not intended by the author.

Cover Design by X-Potion Designs

Cover photo by jackson photografix

Dedication:

To my readers—I am so lucky to have you in my corner.

Thanks for reading.

Chapter One

The bar was dead.

Granted, it was only noon and Mason just opened the doors, but usually he had a small lunch crowd—the people who came in for burgers and fries before they went back to work. Or there were the ones who had beer for their liquid meal.

Here it was, fifteen minutes after opening, and Mason hadn't yet heard a peep.

Not that he was complaining. Closing last night had been hell, and the sandpaper in his eyes was rough as shit. It was past time he got another body in here. He had a cook/dishwasher in back, but he kept it to a bare minimum on the bar. When he could, he worked by himself.

After wiping down tables that he'd just cleaned the night before, Mason tossed the towel onto the bar and then made his way to the small stage. He picked up the guitar that he'd left there, sat on a stool and then plucked a few keys.

He only played around with the damn thing but it was relaxing. He used to want to take lessons, but when he worked full-time for his family restaurants, he hadn't had the time. Now he realized trying to teach himself wasn't as easy as he thought.

A slight thud came from the direction of the door, as if it stuck, and then the familiar creaking sound. He needed to get that fixed. Just another thing to add to his growing to-do list.

A list he actually loved, because he loved his bar. Creekside was the first thing Mason bought for himself. The first place that was his and his alone—not something his father built and wanted for Mason.

His fingers still moved lightly across the strings as a man walked in. He'd never seen the guy before. He definitely wasn't a Blackcreek local. Mason hadn't been here too long himself, but the crew that he had coming in and out was normally consistent, and this guy just didn't have the look of a local.

His hair was a dark blond, the top parted to hang partly off one side of his forehead. That wasn't what caught Mason's eye, though; it was his jawline. Strong, like it was cut out of stone. It was probably the sexiest jawline he'd ever seen.

It was an early June day, yet he wore a pair of black slacks and a button-up shirt—short sleeves, so it fit the weather. It just wasn't what most of his customers wore. His bar as more of a blue collar establishment, which is exactly what Mason wanted for it.

He had long, cut muscles in his forearms. Mason had always had a thing for arms, especially strong, hairy ones like this guy had.

He was slightly shorter than Mason himself, with a clean-shaven face and bitter eyes. Huh. This man could be interesting.

"She needs to be tuned. She's not really far off, but I can hear it in the notes." He nodded toward Mason as he moved his way.

Definitely interesting. "Oh yeah?"

"Yep. Your sound is a little flat. Check your finger positioning on the fretboard."

Mason cocked his left brow. "Anything else?"

"Shit. I'm sorry." He shook his head. "It's a reflex. I've played instruments my whole life. I teach music. Or, I used to."

Mason watched as the music teacher crossed his arms.

"Sounds like you still teach to me."

He frowned as though Mason's reply threw him. "Move the first finger of your left hand just a little farther from the fret and then try it again."

This time it was Mason who frowned. His teacher didn't notice, his eyes zeroed in on Mason's fingers. He'd spent a minute with the guy and it was already obvious how passionate he was about music. It vibrated off of him, fueling Mason to do as he said, moving his finger and then playing again.

"See? Did you hear the difference there?" he asked.

Mason nodded. "Yeah, I did. Thanks, man." And then he held out his hand. "Mason Alexander."

Mason felt callouses on the ends of the guy's fingers when he shook Mason's hand.

"Gavin Davis."

"Beer?" Mason stood up.

"Yeah, thanks. Guinness." Mason turned to put the acoustic back on the stand when Gavin added, "Do you mind?"

He was itching to play. Mason saw it, though he didn't doubt Gavin had instruments of his own. "Have at it." Mason handed the guitar over. Gavin sat as Mason went over to the bar to fill a glass for him. The soft cords of the guitar started almost immediately. It definitely sounded different than when Mason played.

He walked back toward the stage, glass in hand, setting it on a nearby table before turning a chair backward and sitting in it. Gavin continued to play a song Mason didn't know. Hell, he couldn't even tell where Gavin was in this moment, either. He'd somehow left the bar, and was off playing somewhere else. That's what it looked like, at least. Like Gavin was lost in the music. In love with it in a way Mason had never been in love with anything in his life.

"Sorry. I didn't mean to take over like that. I've been traveling so I haven't played much."

"Don't be. You only gave me a complex. I might never pick up the damn thing again."

Gavin stepped off the stage, grabbed the beer and took a drink. "Mind if I buy her?"

"Hey now." Mason laughed. "You don't even have any guilt for making me feel like shit in my own bar? Just want to buy my guitar, huh?" He nodded to the other chair at the table and Gavin sat down.

"What kind of man would I be if I passed up on that kind of opportunity if it just fell into my lap?" He tugged on the right lobe of his ear and gave a shy smile. Mason couldn't tell if he meant to be flirtatious or not. Mason definitely saw it that way, though.

He hadn't been able to get a read on the guy until now, but whether he realized it or not, Gavin definitely eyed him appreciatively. Mason leaned forward, his arms on the back of the chair. "Not the kind of man I'd be interested in." He loved flirting and wanted to test the waters with Gavin.

Gavin pulled away, and Mason figured he'd read the guy wrong. But then he gave Mason another grin, his eyes running down Mason's body. He was interested, so why pull back? Mason cocked a brow at him, and then damned if Gavin didn't lean his way again, though he still looked a little unsure.

Right as he opened his mouth to say something, there was another creaking sound. *Damn it.* Someone came into the bar. Still, Mason didn't move. He watched Gavin, waiting to see what card he played.

It was Gavin who turned to see who came in before taking a long swallow of his beer. Then another.

Mason waited another second and then stood, walked to the counter and served the couple who just came in.

He wasn't there three minutes before Gavin brought an empty glass over and set it in front of him. "I'm late. I didn't realize the time." He set a bill in front of Mason and added, "I have to go."

And then he did just that.

Oh well. Win some, you lose some.

***

Blackcreek, Colorado.

Gavin Davis never expected to live this close to where he'd grown up. Not since the day his high school boyfriend Braden Roth talked him into leaving. Not that Braden had to convince him much. He'd always known he needed to leave Colorado, he just hadn't had the balls to do it until the bigmouthed, and even bigger headed, man had told him he could.

Braden was good for shit like that. It had meant the world to a teenaged Gavin. He hated to admit he'd needed Braden back then. He'd wanted him for a long time afterward as well. It wasn't that Gavin had been in love with Braden; he just had that kind of personality. One people were attracted to—one that had made Gavin feel normal when he'd always been told he wasn't. And he definitely hadn't been crazy enough to think Braden had been in love with him, but for a while, they'd worked. Hell, he'd never even imagined Braden settling down, yet that was part of the reason he was back right now.

Gavin knocked on the door to the small house. Immediately, someone pulled it open.

"'Bout time you got your ass here, man. Come here." Braden pulled him into a hug and Gavin returned it. His body relaxed, feeling at home after seeing his good friend again.

"So, where is he?" Gavin asked when they separated. "I never thought I'd see the day that Braden Roth would settle down."

"Wes is working today. Come on out back. Jess is playing and I need to watch her."

Braden was not only settled down, but he also had the responsibility of a little girl. This whole thing would take some getting used to.

Gavin followed Braden through the house and out the backdoor. There was a wooden swing set in the yard with a curly-haired girl pumping her legs.

"Wes and I built this for her here, though I'm not really sure why since we live at Wes's place."

"I appreciate you letting me stay here."

"Eh." Braden shrugged. "It's just sitting here anyway. Might as well have someone living in it. I'd been thinking about renting her out anyway. Might as well have a friend staying here." Braden turned toward the little girl. "Come over here, Squirt. I want you to meet my friend I told you about."

Her hair bounced up and down as she jumped off the swing and ran over to them.

"You're uncle Braden's old boyfriend. Uncle Wes is his boyfriend now, though." She crossed her arms, eying Gavin up. He bit back a laugh. Jessie was made of fire. He could see that.

Gavin kneeled down. "I'm Braden's friend. He told me all about you and your Uncle Wes. I couldn't wait to meet you."

Her eyes grew wide, obviously satisfied she didn't have to defend Wes's honor by making sure Gavin didn't come to steal his man.

"Braden says you play instruments. He says you teach kids how to play 'em. Can you teach me?"

Gavin got a pinch in his chest, but he made himself ignore it. "I used to teach. I don't anymore, but I would love to show you how to play."

"Yay!" Jessie squealed before running for the swings again.

Gavin pushed to his feet. "She's like a little tornado. What does she want to play?"

"You haven't seen anything yet, and beats the hell out of me. This is the first I've heard of it."

The two men walked over to the porch and sat in the camp chairs. "Love what you've done with the place," Gavin teased him. Though he was surprised. Braden worked with his hands a lot, and he'd always loved outdoors. He was surprised his friend hadn't done more with the property.

"Funny, asshole. I hadn't lived here too long before I met Wes, and before him, I wasn't home often enough to care what it looked like. Now…well, we don't want to take Jessie away from her home, ya know? It's where she lived with her mom. We think it's important that we stay there."

Gavin ran a hand through his hair, trying to figure out how to respond to that. It was so crazy to hear Braden speak that way. He'd always been the free spirit while Gavin was the band geek, and now here he was, living this family life that Gavin had never come close to having. "You've changed. Grown up."

Braden wrinkled his nose. "If you don't take that back, I'll be forced to kick your ass."

Maybe he hadn't changed too much. Both of them laughed.

"You look good. Got more muscle on you than you used to."

Braden nudged Gavin's arm.

"Fuck off. We can't all be sports-playing firemen." Though, Braden was right. Gavin had started working out more lately. It wasn't something he paid much mind to when he was younger. Now, he realized how much he enjoyed it.

"It's hard being this good."

"Married, huh? Does Wes know what he's getting into, agreeing to a lifetime of dealing with your shit?"

Braden looked at Gavin and grinned. "He wouldn't have it any other way."

Gavin didn't doubt that was true.

"What about you? Do you know what you're going to do? I'm not sure if you realized this, but we have schools in Blackcreek. You can still teach, Gav."

The pinch in his chest came back, only now it multiplied. It was like a fucking sledgehammer. "I don't know what's next. I don't know what I want to *be* next, either. Now's not the time to talk about my shit, though. I still can't believe you're getting hitched. Tell me about your life."

Braden picked up where Gavin left off, talking about Wes and Jessie and how they wanted their relationship to be as official as they could for their little girl. Gavin listened to him, genuinely happy for his friend, but also wondering what in the hell was next for himself.

Chapter Two

"Are you stalking me?" Mason took the chair beside Gavin. People were just starting to fill into the empty spaces for the wedding that would start in just a few minutes. It was a hot day in early June, the sun roasting around them.

Wes and Braden were having a small ceremony, with less than fifty folding white chairs lined up in front of an oversized tree with big, weeping branches that sat in the middle of Noah and Cooper's property.

Gavin glanced his way. "If I was stalking you, wouldn't I be hiding?"

"True." He leaned closer, smelled the light sent of cologne. "You never know with the way you ran the other day." Mason hadn't expected to see Gavin again, figured he'd been passing through town; but it was obvious now that he'd come to town at least for the wedding.

"Ran, huh?" Gavin raised a dark brow at him. "Maybe I just wasn't interested."

Mason laughed at that. He'd seen the look in Gavin's eyes. Saw it now as well, even though it seemed to be muted by a slight shyness. He

13

was interested, attracted at the very least.

The look on Gavin's face changed. Not in a bad way, just contemplative. He was a thinker. Mason could tell that much early on, and he weighed his thoughts right now before replying. Gavin looked up and around them. *Was he in the closet?* No, Mason didn't think so. Newly out, then?

Before he had the chance to speak, the officiate walked to the tree and stood below it. Wes and Braden joined him, Braden in black slacks and a short-sleeved, button down shirt. Wes matched except in contrasting white. Both of them looked casual, with Jessie standing beside them in a long summer dress.

When the service began, Mason turned his attention away from the man beside him as Wes and Braden read the vows they'd written, promising to spend their lives together.

At the end of the ceremony, Braden grabbed Wes's face between his hands and kissed the hell out of him before everyone pushed to their feet, clapping. Mason remembered half-heartedly flirting with Braden when they'd met, but seeing him up there now, it didn't even feel like he was looking at the same man.

Mason turned toward Gavin to finish the conversation they'd started, but Gavin seemed lost in the couple in front of them. He had a far-off look in his eyes and a lonely smile on his face. It was enough to make Mason hold back. Hell, probably even pull off completely. Gavin was dealing with some shit; what, Mason didn't know, but he had enough of his own crap right now to not want to get involved with anyone else's.

***

Gavin sat around the bonfire with Braden, Wes, Mason and two other men he'd been introduced to tonight named Noah and Cooper. It was late. He didn't know how late, but the other wedding guests had left hours before.

Wes's sister brought Jessie home with her. Since Braden and Wes weren't going on their honeymoon until later in the summer, they decided to all sit around drinking tonight instead.

"I about shit my pants when Braden admitted that Wes went home with him that first night. And look at them now," Cooper said and everyone laughed.

It surprised Gavin. "You guys didn't know? Don't tell me you went into the closet?" He knew that was bullshit. Braden never worried what anyone thought, never had. In school, Gavin hadn't been the most popular. Braden never cared, and he'd made it easier for Gavin not to worry about things, either. Gavin couldn't help but be curious as to why Braden being with a man was such a huge surprise for Cooper.

"Hell no." Braden reached over and shoved him, almost making Gavin's chair topple over. Mason, who sat beside him, reached over to steady Gavin. "Just because I don't go around announcing my business doesn't mean I hide. Plus, Coop was so damn busy being shocked at his own sexuality that he latched onto mine rather than dealing with his own shit."

Cooper, Noah, Wes and Braden all laughed, apparently in on a joke that he and Mason weren't a part of.

Braden looked his way. "Cooper had never been with a man before

Noah. It wasn't that he was in the closet, he just—"

"Was waiting for me, only he didn't know it," Noah said. Cooper shook his head, but then leaned over and kissed Noah. Gavin took a drink of his beer.

He'd known he was gay since he was a kid. There had never been a time he didn't know it. Even when he pretended otherwise. "No way."

Mason chuckled, but Cooper was quick to defend himself. "It's not bullshit. It wasn't that I spent my life denying who I was. I'd never even looked at a guy before Noah. I never could have fallen in love with a woman though, either. He cast some kind of voodoo shit on me or something. Couldn't live without me, so he made it so I'm the same way about him."

Everyone laughed, Gavin and Mason included. He liked Braden's friends and could see why he enjoyed spending time with them. They were good men.

"Alright." Braden pushed to his feet. "Hate to break up the party, but I'm drunk and it's my wedding night. If I'm going to spend time with my husband before I pass out, it has to be now." He winked at Wes.

"Yeah, what the hell is up with that? You're spending your wedding night drunk in our spare room." Noah wrapped an arm around Wes's shoulder.

"There's a bed, right? That's all they need," Mason added.

"Truer words have never been spoken," Wes said.

Noah looked at Cooper. "Let's go." He nodded toward the house, and Cooper was on his feet as well. "Sorry it's the couches for you guys, but we put blankets and pillows out for you."

They'd spent the whole night drinking, and all of them where too hammered to drive.

"You guys coming in, or can you get the fire for us?" Noah asked.

Even though tiredness weighed down his muscles, Gavin didn't think he could sleep yet. He had too much on his mind with Braden, his family and figuring out what the hell he was going to do in Blackcreek. He glanced Mason's way. Mason nodded as though he knew what Gavin was asking. "I'll put the fire out before we go in."

"Thanks, man," Noah nodded at him.

Braden put a hand on Gavin's shoulder and squeezed. They'd been through a lot together, the two of them. He was glad to have his friend back in his life.

The four men walked away, leaving Gavin and Mason alone with the sounds of a summer night—the crackle of the fire, crickets and wind through the trees.

It was nice. He didn't realize how much he missed living in a place like this after he'd pretended to belong in the suburbs for so long.

"So." Mason finished off the beer in his hand. "What's the history with you and Braden?"

Ah hell. That question was loaded down with more history than Gavin wanted to go into.

Chapter Three

"Toss me another." Mason nodded toward the cooler, wondering why in the hell he asked Gavin about Braden. All he should be doing was drinking and enjoying the night, and not getting into other people's business.

But then, he'd always been curious. Maybe that's why he made such a good bartender. He liked talking to people. It had made him good in the restaurant business, as well.

Gavin pulled a can from the cooler and handed it to Mason.

"Good friends," Gavin finally answered. "He was my first boyfriend when we were in high school. We moved away together afterward."

"No shit?"

Gavin nodded, looking a little lost in thought. "It was strange seeing him with Wes today. With their little girl and all their relatives. The acceptance. It's a beautiful thing."

Now they were getting somewhere. The edge to Gavin's voice told

Mason that he hadn't experienced the same kind of acceptance. In some ways, Mason hadn't, either. Not that his family cared he was gay. They never had, but there were many ways to make someone feel bad about the person they were, even when it wasn't done on purpose. Obligation was a damn heavy weight to carry.

"So, you came in for the wedding and then you're heading home? Where is home, anyway?"

Gavin sighed and dropped his head back, looking at the sky. Mason loved the night—the darkness, and the little specks of light up there. The stall in Gavin told him he'd just hit a sour subject. Or maybe he just thought Mason was a nosy son of a bitch—which he was.

"Hell, I don't know where home is. I don't really know what I'm doing, either."

The words echoed through Mason, swam around and made a home there. No, they'd been there already, because he felt the same. He always had. It's why he moved to Blackcreek and bought the bar in the first place.

"I used to teach music at a high school. I lost my job. I guess I didn't really lose it since I just walked away, but…" Gavin took a drink, and Mason had a feeling the alcohol gave him a looser tongue than he'd normally have. "It's all I've ever done. And I loved it, in a way. I've always loved music, but I think I always knew I didn't belong where I was anyway. It was never real. Hell, I'm drunk. I don't know what I'm saying. The point is I'm renting Braden's house. Not sure how long I'll be here or what I'm going to do."

There was a story there. Mason heard it in the tone of his voice, but really it wasn't any of his business.

Gavin stood, stretched. When he did his shirt rose, showing Mason muscular abs and a trail of dark hair. The man was sexy, but that's not what had his mind running right now. Gavin had said he didn't know what he was saying, but Mason understood it. He felt it, because despite having a family who loved and accepted him, he never felt like he belonged, either.

Turns out he didn't—only everyone except for Mason himself had been in on it until recently.

"You ever bartend?" he asked on a whim.

Gavin looked down at him and cocked a brow. "No."

"It's not teaching, but if you're looking for something to do, I have a position open. Could use a little help. The pay's not great, the hours suck, and it would only be part-time, but we have a hell of a good time down there." He winked.

"Even though I've never tended bar before?" Gavin smirked. Mason couldn't tell if he wanted to look as sexy as he did or if he was just drunk and couldn't smile straight. Either way, he liked the view.

"Eh, I know your friends so I'll give you a chance. I'll give you a book I have on mixed drinks to go over."

"Homework and studying? Maybe it's not too different from teaching. Sounds like it's right up my alley."

Not even close to teaching but that was okay. "Come down to the bar in the next few days and I'll give you some paperwork to fill out."

Gavin paused, looked down at him. He had an expression in his eyes that Mason couldn't read. Or maybe it was the alcohol again. Who knew?

Gavin held out his hand and they shook before he pulled Mason to his feet. Their bodies were close. There was nothing like the feel of a hard, masculine body against his own.

"Thanks for the chance. I really appreciate it," Gavin told him but didn't back away. All Mason could smell was fire and he suddenly wanted the scent of man. It was strange, because for Mason, it made his body come alert. Gavin didn't seem to notice, though. It was like he didn't clue into things like that. It had been the same at the bar.

"I'm horny when I'm drunk. You're not doing me any favors standing so close." As soon as the words left his mouth, Mason realized how they sounded. He meant them as a joke, but considering he just offered the guy a job, it probably wasn't the best time to make a sex joke. "Hey, I didn't mean—"

"Guess you should have thought about that before you decided to become my boss." Gavin gave him a mischievous smirk, and Mason let out a relieved breath. He'd taken it the way Mason meant.

"Hell, I take it back. Or you're fired. Whatever works better." They both laughed, and it felt good. Real. "Come on, let's get this fire put out."

Mason still chuckled as they took care of the fire and then headed inside for some much needed sleep.

***

Gavin's nerves were on edge as the phone rang. It shouldn't be like that. He shouldn't dread and worry about talking to his family, but yet he did. His fault? Their fault? Probably a combination of all of them because he didn't push, never had, and they hadn't been willing to let their beliefs evolve out of love for him, either.

"Hello?" The soft voice of his mother drifted through the line.

"Hi. It's Gavin."

"Gavin!" The tone excitedly went up a few octaves. "It's so good to hear from you. How are you?" Gavin settled against the back of the couch. *Still gay...*

"I'm good. I wanted to let you know that I'm settled into Blackcreek. I've already found a job."

She sighed, and he could tell she wasn't happy. Wait until she found out what kind of job he'd gotten.

"Did you ask the school to take you back like we spoke about? Apologize for what you did? I'm sure with your record they could excuse you."

Gavin ignored her question, because what the hell had he done? Nothing wrong. He'd tried to help a kid, that's all. "It's at a bar. I'm going to be a bartender." Guilt slammed into him because he knew this would upset her, yet he said it anyway. It's probably the reason he did.

"Do you think that's a good idea? You need to surround yourself with people who follow the Lord, Gavin."

And people who go into a bar obviously can't be that kind of person. Why the hell did it have to be that way?

Gavin's defenses took over, controlled his mouth. Growing up he would have apologized, hidden who he was or completely walked away.

22

Guilt would have eaten through him for his older parents, who tried so hard to have him. Who were stuck in their beliefs and who he *did* know loved him. Hell, even a few months ago he wouldn't have shared his plans. He would have kept who he was private. But where had that gotten him? With parents who still worried about his soul, a life alone, and having his career taken away from him.

Now, all he could think about was what he'd lost. The things he didn't have. The fact that he was thirty years old and didn't know what he wanted because he always tried to be who they needed him to be.

And right or wrong, it made him angry. "I'm staying at Braden's house and—"

"I don't think you're making wise decisions. You've lost your job because of your choices, and that boy, he…"

Was the first person to tell Gavin it was okay to be who he is. Was the first person in his life to accept him without praying for his soul and telling him he would go to hell. "He doesn't live here anymore. He lives with his husband and their daughter. Even if he didn't, he's no different than me. And I didn't lose my job because of choices I made. It was taken away from me because of ignorance."

"The bible says—"

"Don't! I can't do this." Gavin shoved to his feet just as the quiet cries started. That was his mom—she got hurt, worried, sad, cried. His dad got angry and preached.

"We just worry about you so much. You're our only son and we love you."

And he knew they did.

Gavin's guilt started gnawing on his bones again—not over who he was, but by him baiting her. He'd said those things knowing they would upset her. He paced Braden's living room. Well—his living room, he guessed. "I know. I'm sorry. I love you, too. How is he…? Dad?"

He heard movement through the line and he imagined his mom wiping her tears, trying to be strong. "As good as can be expected. He has his good days and his bad. Dementia is a horrible disease. I know he'd like to see you, though. He misses you, even if he can't always express it."

The thing was, as much as it hurt to see them, Gavin missed his family, as well.

Chapter Four

"You're never going to be able to forgive me, are you?" Isaac sat on Mason's couch as Mason leaned against the wall by the door. He shouldn't have been shocked to open his door and see his ex-standing there. It wasn't the first time he'd driven down from Denver since Mason moved to Blackcreek. In the beginning, it was when he wanted to fuck. Ever since Mason completely called things off, it was to give him hell.

Isaac scratched his knee while Mason decided how to respond to the question. He'd spent three years of his life with this man. They'd been great together in a lot of ways. Neither required a lot as far as relationships went. They were fairly open, put work first, and were happy that way. Then Mason discovered Isaac lied to him the same way his family had, and suddenly Isaac couldn't leave him alone.

Obviously getting antsy, Isaac pushed the sleeves up on his shirt. Here it was early summer and he wore a long-sleeved button down.

"It's not a matter of forgiveness. Was I pissed? Of course. In some ways I still am." Mason crossed his arms.

"It wasn't my place to tell you. It—"

"I was your lover, and your closest friend. It *was* your place. I never would have kept secrets from you. Not something that big. Not when you know how I feel about lying." Not when he knew Mason already questioned who he was. The anger started to rise in him again, heat scorching his body. How could his family, and lover, keep something so big from him?

Mason shook his head, tired of dealing with it all. He'd spent most of his life feeling different, following dreams that weren't his, and he was finally moving on. "If it's the words you need to hear, then I forgive you. But that doesn't change anything."

Half of Isaac's mouth rose. "Yes it does." He stood and walked over to Mason, didn't stop until their bodies touched. Mason didn't move away. "I want you back."

"You can't have me." They eyed each other, neither man backing down.

Isaac cursed. "I didn't know what to do. I thought it was the right thing."

Mason didn't doubt that. "I know, but it doesn't change anything. That wasn't me—the life we had in Denver. I don't want the same shit you do." Even when they'd been happily together Mason had known that. He'd just been willing to pretend back then. He wasn't willing any longer.

"Right now, all I want is to fuck you." Isaac reached for him but Mason grabbed his wrist in a tight hold.

Wanted to play that way, did he? Mason didn't let go of Isaac's wrist. He leaned in closer. "You didn't get to call the shots on that before and you don't get to now, either. When I'm in the mood to be fucked, it won't be you I'm telling to do it anymore. Now, I have to get to the bar." Mason let go and slid from between Isaac and the wall. His ex groaned.

"You're killing me, Mason."

"You never did like to lose." He grabbed his wallet from the table and pushed it into his back pocket.

Isaac laughed. "I'm not giving up."

Mason knew that was coming. Like he said, Isaac never liked to lose, and the fact that Mason walked away was a loss to the man. "I didn't figure you would, but you know I don't back down, either."

Isaac adjusted himself and then opened the door, signaling for Mason to step out. He did, followed by Isaac. They both walked over to their vehicles—Isaac to his Lexus and Mason to his Expedition. "Hey," Mason called to him. Regardless of what went down between them, Mason still considered Isaac his friend.

Isaac turned to look at him before Mason spoke again. "I really do forgive you. We've been friends too long not to."

"And for what it's worth, I'm sorry."

"I know."

"I'm still not giving up, though. Oh, and Mom and Dad told me to tell you they want us to come over for dinner next Saturday. They miss the two of us spending time together with them." Isaac winked, got into his car and drove away.

They'd grown up together. When Isaac's parents died, he got even closer to Mason's. He'd called Mason's parents Mom and Dad ever since

Mason could remember.

He shook his head, not surprised Isaac would use everything he had in his arsenal, even Mason's parents to conquer him.

***

Gavin watched as Mason squinted and then blew out a deep breath while shaking his head. "Are you trying to get me drunk when I have a shift that starts in two hours? Too much vodka." Damn it. It was the first drink he made and he'd wanted to get it right.

"It tasted good to me."

Mason set the glass down and then stood beside Gavin. "Less is sometimes more. You don't want it to be overpowering. Think of it like...hell, I don't know, you're playing the guitar or something."

With that, Gavin laughed. "That doesn't make any sense at all."

"Yes it does—or at least pretend it does. There's a fine art to making a good drink. You'll learn it, but I'm assuming music is the same way. You walked into the bar that first day and heard something in the notes that I didn't. A good bartender knows how to use just the right amounts to give the perfect flavor."

Gavin looked at Mason, Mason at Gavin, before both of them let out loud bursts of laughter. His gut hurt before he could finally calm down enough to speak. "That was the biggest piece of bullshit I've ever heard."

"Fuck you. You're fired. I'm trying here."

It was Gavin's first day. The bar would be open soon, and though he and Mason would be working together, he was nervous. Which made him feel crazy. What was there to be nervous about? But it felt like this was his new beginning, or he wanted it to be. Wanted to really find out who he was and experience new things. The last thing he wanted to do was fail at any of them. It didn't matter if he was making drinks or teaching children, Gavin wanted to do it well.

"Maybe it would help if I drank more." Gavin turned, leaned against the bar and crossed his arms.

"I just got drunk with you the other night."

"And it didn't take much to get me that way. It's never really been something I'm into. Yeah, I have a beer when I'm watching a game or something, but that's about it."

There was a pause on Mason's end before he turned the same direction as Gavin and nudged him with his arm. "Nah, you don't have to be an alcoholic to make a good drink. Yeah, it's different as night and day from teaching kids music, but like anything, it just takes a little practice. What's really on your mind?"

Gavin smirked, trying to pretend Mason didn't just hit the nail on the head. And wondering why the man would care what Gavin dealt with. "I'd heard bartenders were like barbers and liked to pretend to be a therapist, but I didn't expect it so soon."

"If you can't trust your bartender, who can you trust?" There was a teasing edge to Mason's deep voice. He liked the lightness of the man. It was a good contrast to the storm inside of him. The conversation he'd had with his mom weighed heavier on Gavin than he'd expected.

"Eh, it's nothing really," Gavin said. It was a lie, and when he'd moved to Blackcreek he told himself he was over lying about anything.

"No, fuck it. It's not. My dad has dementia. I haven't seen my parents as much as I should. They don't live far from here, which should be a good thing given the circumstances, but we have a complicated relationship, to say the least."

"I'll drink to that," Mason replied, though he didn't take a drink of anything.

Gavin pushed off the bar and faced Mason. "I've lost my job and my father is losing his mind. Coming here, seeing Braden with his husband and his kid..." He shrugged. "I guess it makes me see things differently. I'm in my thirties and I don't feel like I have anything to show for my life." Hell, in a lot of ways, he didn't really have a life. He'd had a career he'd loved, but that had been all. He'd given his life to teaching, which in a lot of ways he didn't regret, but when had he taken time for himself?

"I hear ya. That's what this bar is—something for me. It's the one thing I have that I want and no one else had a hand in." Mason seemed to think for a second before he smirked and nodded his head at Gavin. "Hey...you ever jumped out of a plane before?"

Gavin eyed him, wondering where that came from. "That came out of thin air." Pun intended. Mason rolled his eyes and Gavin continued, "No...not really sure I want to, either."

"Let's do it. It's a rush. There's nothing like the clarity you get on your life when you're falling thousands of feet through the air. You want to figure out your life, it's one of the best ways."

For some reason, Gavin didn't have to think about his answer. The only way for him to find what he really wanted in life was to get out and live it. "Name the time and place, boss."

Chapter Five

Mason had gone skydiving twice in his life, both times when he'd needed a little clarity—the first right before he moved to Blackcreek, and the second a couple months ago when he found out he'd been lied to his whole life.

He hadn't planned on going again when he asked Gavin, but something about the way he'd spoken to Mason prompted the question. Mason knew what it felt like for your life to suddenly seem as though it wasn't what you thought it was—as though you didn't really know what direction to go. He saw that feeling mirrored in Gavin. Even though he didn't know Gavin well, he understood him on that level and wanted to help.

Plus, jumping out of a plane was fun as hell, and he was actually looking forward to the chance to spend a little more time with Gavin. Mason had this urge to figure him out, and he couldn't yet.

They'd planned the trip for Sunday since it was one of the two days Mason took off at the bar. Gavin had worked a few shifts during the week and seemed to be fitting in well, which he was happy about. Mason took Creekside seriously. He'd always been somewhat of a workaholic, and that didn't change when he bought his bar.

Mason pulled up at Gavin's house to see him waiting on the porch.

"Hey. Thanks for picking me up," Gavin told him as he climbed into Mason's vehicle.

They had about an hour and a half drive ahead of them, and though it wasn't too early, they'd both worked late at the bar last night. As Mason started to pull away, he spoke. "No problem. There's coffee in the thermos if you want some. Black with sugar."

Gavin raised a brow at him. "No creamer? Can we stop by Starbucks or something?"

"What? Get out." He stopped driving. "No talk about fake coffee when you're with me."

"Ah, don't tell me you're one of those? Real men can't drink good coffee?"

Mason started driving again. "Did you just insinuate that my coffee isn't good?"

"Maybe it's because you're a good bartender... You know, you make good drinks so you make shit coffee. Can't be good at everything, ya know?"

"Fuck you. My coffee *and* my drinks are good. Don't be jealous because I'm a man of many talents. I'm not selfish. I can teach you all my tricks if you want."

Gavin leaned back, his head resting against the seat as he turned to look Mason's way. His eyes looked tired, and slightly red. He hadn't shaved today, and Mason liked the dark hair on his jaw. He wore jeans that hugged his legs, and a t-shirt pulled tight against his chest. He had this innocence to him that Mason could practically feel, but at the same time Mason sensed more beneath the surface. He wasn't sure what exactly it was, but it intrigued him.

"Are you going to watch the road so we don't kill ourselves before we get to jump out of the plane?" Gavin smirked. "And are we really going to go there? With the '*all* my tricks' thing? I'm not sure I'm awake enough yet to flirt."

Mason shook his head and got his eyes back on the road where they belonged. "Fucker." Still, he couldn't help but smile.

***

They were quiet for most of the drive and Gavin was thankful for it. Not that he didn't want to speak to Mason, but because it wasn't every day that he jumped out of a plane.

Both excitement and nerves made his muscles twitch and his body feel overworked. Part of that was probably all the shit he had on his mind as well. He hadn't talked to his mom since their conversation almost a week ago. He started working as a bartender, something he never saw himself doing. His mind had been running since the day he was forced to walk away from the career he'd given his life to. Deciding to go skydiving intensified it.

"Second thoughts?" Mason asked as he killed the engine in the parking lot of the skydiving facility.

Soon, he would be jumping out of a plane. Falling, flying, letting go. Which was exactly what he wanted in his life—to really live it and discover who Gavin Davis really was. "Not a chance."

Gavin got out of the vehicle, Mason right behind him. They went inside, and watched a training video first. He had his arms crossed the whole time, the fingers of one hand tapping on the other arm because he couldn't keep still.

He'd never done something like this before in his life, never even considered it, and suddenly he couldn't wait.

After the video finished they got suited up and put their harnesses on. It was a short drive in a company truck to take them where the actual plane would take off.

The muscles in Gavin's body kept getting tighter and tighter. He'd always lived his life sort of tense, but right now he felt incased in cement. Rigid.

When Gavin, Mason, the two instructors and the pilot were all in the tiny plane, it started down the runway, door still open.

"I've never flown before!" Gavin had to shout so Mason could hear him over the noise from the plane.

"Are you fucking kidding me? You've never been in a plane and the first time you do, you decide to jump out of one?"

"Looks that way!" Gavin turned away, his left leg bouncing up and down against Mason's.

"Holy shit, you're something else."

Out of the corner of his eye, Gavin saw Mason shaking his head but he didn't reply.

The ride was bumpy and loud. His ears popped the higher they went.

Before he knew it, they were telling him it was time.

Gavin didn't know how they all fit as the four men moved around, one instructor attaching himself to Mason and the other to Gavin.

"Who goes first?" One of the instructors called out.

Mason looked at Gavin as though waiting for him to answer. Gavin felt a tickle on the back of his neck. Nerves started to take root, deeper inside him, but not enough to make him back down.

He nodded at Mason, who threw a sexy smile at him before moving to the open door. He couldn't hear what they were saying to each other, but then suddenly Mason and his instructor were tumbling backward out of the plane. His stomach dropped with them as he watched them fall through the air.

"We're up. Backward on the count of three!" His instructor told him. "One,"

Oh shit.

"Two."

What the fuck was I thinking?

"Three!"

Freedom.

Wind rushed around him, rumbled loudly though his ear. Fear didn't fit here. It felt like he was alive for the first time—invincible yet small and breakable at the same time. He could live forever. He could die in a second. None of it mattered. Nothing did. Not the fact that his dad was losing his mind. That his mom would be alone. That his parents prayed for him daily because they thought he would spend eternity burning in hell.

His job didn't matter. Life was short, could end at any second, and he hadn't even lived it. Not really. And why?

It was a rush like nothing Gavin had ever experienced before.

Suddenly Gavin's whole body jerked and he was yanked upward as the parachute opened.

And then nothing but quiet peace, the world at his fingertips.

When his feet hit the ground, all Gavin could think about was flying again. He wanted to spend the rest of his life that way.

Chapter Six

"I've never felt anything like that." Gavin shook out his hands and then held them up to Mason.

They were trembling.

"It's adrenaline. I feel it rushing through my body. I can't turn the shit off."

Mason watched as Gavin paced outside of the building. They'd finished their jump a while ago, and were about to head back to his vehicle. Gavin hadn't stopped moving the whole time.

"Do you want to? Turn it off?"

"My legs feel like they could go out from under me at any second. My heart is a fucking jackhammer. I want to burst out of my skin, but not in a bad way." He stopped in front of Mason. "No, I don't want to turn it off."

That's what he wanted to hear. "I felt like that my first time. You're not going to want to be cooped up in the truck while I drive all the way home. Boulder's close. We can head over there, hang out, maybe hike some trails or something."

For the first time since they touched the ground again, Gavin stopped moving. "Yeah?" The surprise in Gavin's voice came unexpected.

"Yeah, sure. It's not like I'd pass up a chance to spend a day outdoors when I'm usually locked in the bar all day." He nodded toward his vehicle. "Let's go."

Still, Mason called Creekside to check on things. It was a habit that he knew he should get out of. They could handle it. His employees had his phone number. Still, he called and stopped by more than he should on his days off.

It didn't take them long to get to the park. Mason had been here before. It was a little out of town, and had not only hiking trails but also sports and other activities on the other side.

They'd grabbed some food, water and ice before they arrived and put them in a small, insulated bag that Mason had with him, then tossed it into a backpack.

"You seem awfully prepared. I'm starting to think you had this planned." Gavin leaned against the door as Mason walked over to his side.

"You figured me out. It's my MO. I find sexy men, give them jobs, make them jump out of planes with me and then lure them onto hikes where I can take advantage of them." He leaned in, invaded Gavin's space. "Or let them take advantage of me."

Gavin pushed away before heading for the trail, leading through the trees. "Makes sense. One question, though. Why go through all that trouble? I mean, is it that hard for you to get laid?"

"You're a funny man." Mason stepped up beside him. "More likely excuse is being busy. When I'm working, that's typically all that's on my mind. And I'm always working." Which was only a partial lie. He thought about sex, often. But he also kept busy. Even before the bar, when he worked for the restaurant chain, his life mostly consisted of work.

He and Isaac had that in common. They'd worked well in that respect. Worked hard, and when they had time, fucked hard, too. They were committed to each other but also committed to their work. They'd been exclusive, but their first priorities had always been their career—a career Mason had been more than willing to leave behind, even if it took a lie to finally make him do it for good.

"Really?" Gavin glanced at him as they rounded a rock and continued on their way up. "You don't seem the type. Not that I'm surprised you take your work seriously, you just…"

"Eh, things haven't always been the way they are now," Mason finished before Gavin could continue. "I grew up thinking my life would always be one thing—my parents own a few very high-end restaurants. I grew up around them, working with them, always knowing that one day they would be mine."

"How high-end?" Gavin asked.

"The kind where I worked in a suit every day. I started to run the main restaurant in Denver. It's the kind of place where people drop big money on a meal." He never fucking got that. His parents were the same way. Mason could think of a million other things he'd rather spend money on than a meal that left him still feeling hungry and a bottle of champagne.

"But you didn't want it?" He nudged Mason, which made him stop. Gavin pulled a bottle of water from the pack on Mason's back and then they were on their way again.

Not wanting it was an understatement. "I never really felt like I fit. I grew up well, never went without anything. My parents loved me and supported me. Never had a problem with me being gay, but…" It had never felt right. He'd never wanted the same things they did. He'd always felt different.

"You're lucky. Not everyone has it that easy."

Mason didn't take offense. Gavin was right. He'd known a lot of people in this life that had friends or family who had a problem with their sexuality. He'd never get that, why one person cared who the hell someone else loved. "That doesn't always change how you feel, though."

"No…no, it doesn't." Leaves and branches cracked beneath their feet as they walked. Neither of them spoke, but he sensed the heaviness of the moment. Sensed the heaviness pulsating from Gavin. Things must have been pretty bad with his family, and that reminded Mason how lucky he was in so many ways. Why couldn't he just accept that?

Finally, Gavin spoke. "We have a few things in common."

If Gavin thought he was leaving it there, the man had another think coming.

***

"Like what?" Mason asked.

Gavin's first instinct—not to reply—hit him, but he still had all that adrenaline pumping through him from the jump and his epiphany that he wanted to spend his life flying instead of keeping himself chained to certain ideas of what his life should be. It was those things that made him admit, "Seeing your life a certain way. Having people who love you expect something specific from you."

"And what do they expect?" Mason grabbed the bottle of water from Gavin's hand and took a drink.

His legs burned slightly from the climb, mixed with the intensity of his jump. "To be a good Christian boy. To repent, find a nice woman to marry, have children and raise them in the church. It's the only way to spend the afterlife with my parents instead of burning in hell."

Damn, he couldn't believe he'd just said that. The only person he'd ever really talk to about it before was Braden.

Mason didn't stop walking so neither did Gavin. "No shit?" he asked. "So your family doesn't support you?"

Gavin thought for a second. "That's a tough question. They love me. I know they do. They would never disown me, but they don't support me, either. It's not the angry kind of non-support." It was the kind that made his chest ache. The kind filled with guilt when he thought of his parents' tears and their bone-deep belief that the son they loved would go to Hell.

"Which makes it even worse...."

Mason's words hung in the air, and Gavin somehow knew he didn't need to tell Mason that he was right. The kind of—hell, what felt like betrayal—that came from love, no matter how wrong it was, made the pain even greater.

Chapter Seven

Mason decided to let the heavy conversation go as they continued the climb. Heavy didn't typically go hand-in-hand with one of the first times he hung out with someone.

It didn't typically go with him at all.

They talked about nothing and everything at the same time. A little over an hour after talking about Gavin's family, they took a break to eat before they started up again.

About four o'clock, Mason climbed around a massive rock and around a few trees before turning around to Gavin. "We made it."

Gavin stumbled on a root. Mason held out a hand for Gavin, which he grabbed, allowing Mason to steady him as he pulled himself up. He didn't speak for a minute, his eyes slowly taking in the sight in front of them.

"Damn, it's incredible up here."

Mason looked out at the mountains, trees and sky—green and blue as far as he could see. Gavin was right. The view was incredible.

"Makes you feel small."

Mason nudged him. "We jumped out of an airplane today and *this* makes you feel small?"

Gavin chuckled. "They both do, in a way. Skydiving is a rush, though. You don't get to take the time to just be in the moment, to think about shit. Up here, you can think; makes you realize there really is a whole world out there, and that *does* make you feel small."

Yeah, he got where Gavin came from on that one. "It's a good kind of small, if that makes sense." And then, "Look at us, jumping out of planes, hiking and contemplating life. You trying to get me centered, or something?"

Gavin laughed the way Mason hoped he would. The man had a sexy smile, and Mason liked putting it on his face.

"It's funny, you climb all the way up, just to turn around and go back down." The softness in Gavin's voice told Mason he wasn't ready to leave, which was fine by him.

"Sit down. No one said we had to go anywhere yet."

Gavin looked Mason's way and raised a brow. "Bossy, aren't you?"

"You ain't seen nothin' yet. And just think, I actually *am* your boss. What should I do with all that power?"

"Are you going to make me regret taking this job? I really wanted to like you, but you know it's impossible to like asshole bosses. The man always trying to hold us down and all."

Mason laughed. "Shut up and sit down. My legs are tired."

"Bossy," he heard Gavin playfully mumble, but then he sat down, leaning against a rock. Mason went down beside him. It was Gavin who spoke first. "I wish I had my guitar out here with me."

A light wind brushed over his skin. It was quiet, peaceful and quiet. "Yeah, me, too." Not just because he wanted to hear Gavin play, either. Just seeing him with a guitar the one time showed Mason how much music helped set Gavin free.

"Why'd you leave your job, man?" Gavin had obviously loved it.

Gavin answered his question with one of his own. "If your family supported you, why didn't you feel like you fit with them?"

Eh, that was an easy one. "Because I didn't. Most of it was what I said earlier; they wanted one thing from me and I wanted another. It was hard, though, when you have a good family who would do anything for you. It makes it tough to let them down. Most people would be happy to be handed the reigns to a million-dollar business."

Gavin picked up a small pebble, rolling it around in his hands. "Not you?"

"Yes and no. I appreciated it, but I didn't want it. It's hard to explain. I wanted something I created for myself, ya know? Hell, when I moved to Blackcreek I didn't even let anyone know who I am. I didn't want to be associated with Alexander's. I wanted Creekside to be something Mason did on his own—not Mason Alexander's experiment. That's how I had to twist it, though—that I was just a man who owned some restaurants, left them and moved here, when really, to my family, it *was* my experiment. The plan had originally been to move back to Denver for the restaurants. I love my family. I always have. But I still always felt different. Then one day, I found out why."

When Mason didn't continue, Gavin lightly pushed him with his elbow. "Are you going to tell me why?"

Mason got a cramp in his gut. The words were still hard to say, even though he wasn't sure if it should be as difficult as it was. "Because I don't. Not really. Stumbled upon paperwork I shouldn't have. Oh, hey, we forgot to tell you, son. You're not really our son. You belong to a drug addict your mom went to college with." Maybe at his age, it shouldn't matter. Maybe he shouldn't care. His family loved him, raised him, and treated him well. Did blood really matter? To him, it did.

The fact that they'd never told him mattered. That Isaac had found out but didn't tell him, either. And knowing that his mom got clean when he was ten years old and he'd still not gotten so much as a phone call from her mattered as well.

It hurt like hell.

***

Damn, Gavin definitely hadn't expected that. He could tell there was more to the story as well. "Do you know where she is? Have you contacted her? Asked your parents about her?"

Mason turned his head toward Gavin. "I don't think so. My turn is over. Aren't we playing the get-to-know-you game? Tit for tat, Teach. Don't tell me I have to explain to you the rules of the game."

Gavin leaned his head back against the tree, waiting to feel himself clam up, waiting to feel the urge to pull back because Mason was trying to find out too much about him.

It didn't happen.

"They found out I was gay."

"How did they not know you are gay?"

Gavin shrugged. "Am I supposed to go around with a sign on my forehead? Maybe my back, too?" He tried to stand but Mason grabbed his arm and pulled him back down.

"Don't. You know that's not what I meant."

And he did. "I was...discreet. I taught at a Christian school. My dad's a teacher, and Mom was before she had me. All I ever wanted to do was teach, and I didn't want to threaten that, so I kept my business to myself. It's not as if I had a lot of time to date, anyway."

Mason still held Gavin's wrist as they sat there. He liked the feel of the strong hand on him.

"And?"

Gavin almost called him bossy again but figured this wasn't the best time. The ache in his stomach got worse. Spilling his guts to a man he just met wasn't his idea of a good time, yet he found himself willing to do it anyway. "I noticed a boy being picked on. We started talking. I wanted to help him. The kid admitted he's gay. I gave him my support, his parents didn't like it. There went my job. That's the basics of it. Tried to help a kid, lost my job."

Wasn't that his job as a teacher? To help? Wasn't that his job as a human being? Apparently not where they'd been concerned.

When Mason didn't reply, Gavin looked his way. Mason's green eyes pinned him, trapped him with what looked like respect burning there. Gavin wanted that look, wanted someone who got it, and Mason didn't have to say it for Gavin to know he did. "You did the right thing."

"I know." And in reality he did, but from there on, he'd done nothing to fight.

Mason licked his lips, and Gavin found himself wanting to be the one to do it. Mason was a sexy man. His short hair looked soft. Gavin wanted to grab it, but initiating things wasn't typically his game.

"I want to kiss you. Not sure it's a good idea, though."

Gavin wasn't, either, but he wanted it. Right now, he really fucking wanted it. "It is—a good idea." The words hardly left his mouth before Mason's lips touched his, gentle and slow. His hand moved from Gavin's wrist to cup the side of his face as he teased Gavin's mouth open.

It had been much too long since Gavin kissed a man. The second their tongues touched things went from zero to sixty in no time flat. All he could think about was wanting more.

Mason's hand pulled his hair as his tongue pushed into Gavin's mouth. Urgent. Hungry. Incredible.

Gavin didn't notice him move, but suddenly Mason sat on top of him, straddling his legs. His body was hard, his thighs thick with corded muscle as they hugged Gavin's body.

Mason grabbed Gavin's hand and put it on his jean-covered erection. "I've been hard for you all day. I'm really not sure this is a good idea. It's your call. Tell me to stop if you want me to. No hard feelings. This is completely separate from the job." And then his mouth owned Gavin's again.

Gavin wanted to be owned.

He should take Mason up on his chance to pull the brakes on things. He worked for the guy, and they both obviously had big shit going on in their lives. But he wanted this. He wanted Mason. Wanted a man. And he hadn't taken something for himself in too damn long.

Gavin squeezed Mason's dick, rubbed it through the fabric. "Do you have any condoms?" Gavin let that be his answer. He dropped his head backward when Mason bit his neck. Hard.

And he fucking loved it.

"No... Don't need them. I'm going to suck you off. Tell me before you come and I'll watch you blow all over your own stomach. Maybe make you eat it off yourself and then you'll suck me and I'll do the same for you."

Gavin's prick jerked, much too stifled behind his zipper. He wanted what Mason said. Wanted it so much he feared that the second his cock slipped into Mason's warm, wet mouth, he'd lose it.

Mason crawled between Gavin's legs. They both had dirt all over them but he didn't give a shit.

Gavin went to unbutton his shorts but Mason shoved his hands away. "This is my game. I get to do what I want."

And then it was Mason's hands unbuttoning Gavin's pants, sliding his zipper down. Pulling his jeans open. Leaning over, he nuzzled his face into Gavin's crotch, sucked him through his underwear and his cock jerked again. Ached with need.

"Oh, fuck."

Gavin grabbed the back of Mason's head, ready to hold him down if he had to, when he heard it—"We're almost there. Not much farther, Tammy."

"Shit!" Mason groaned against him but didn't move. Gavin's pulse kicked up. He pushed Mason away, fumbling with his pants as he tried to get them closed again. Mason rolled, now lying in the dirt, his head next to a rock and his arm thrown over his face. The second Gavin got his shorts button and zipped, two people appeared.

"Hey! Gorgeous view, isn't it?" The woman asked.

Mason didn't answer, leaving Gavin to play nice with the people who just kept him from getting off.

Chapter Eight

Mason and Gavin waited it out for a while, but the other couple wasn't leaving. The longer they sat there, Mason could see the change in Gavin—see him starting to overthink things. Or hell, maybe that was him. Or he was imagining things. All he knew was, despite the hunger eating him alive and the ache in his dick, the mood was dead.

"You ready to head back down?" Mason asked him. When Gavin agreed, he stood and started the hike back down. He didn't take the time to dust off the dirt from his clothes. Mason didn't really give a shit about that. He was horny and in a bad mood.

The trip down went faster than the trip up. Their drive home was the same. They talked off and on, not about anything important. During the downtime, Mason found himself thinking about the strangest things. Not how much he'd wanted a dick in his mouth earlier, but about the things Gavin said regarding his life and his family.

Christ, he couldn't imagine being told he would go to Hell—not only because of who he loved, but *from* someone who loved him.

It didn't take much for him to see that Gavin was a good guy. A minute with him was all it took for Mason to realize that, and the thought of people not seeing that made his hands tighten almost painfully on the steering wheel. Mason knew he was lucky. He'd never dealt with that kind of outright homophobia, especially from his own family.

The world really was a fucked up place sometimes.

When he pulled up in front of Gavin's place, he didn't kill the engine.

Gavin unclicked his seatbelt. "Thanks for today. That was...holy shit, we jumped out of a plane together today."

Mason wasn't sure why but that made him laugh. "We did. It clear your head?"

"As much as it could."

"Good." He nodded his head. "I'll give you a call once I figure out the schedule. You're available any day, right?"

"I am. Listen...about earlier," Gavin said, "We were both horny, almost got lucky, but hell, maybe with working together, things ended up the way they should be."

No, things didn't feel like they ended up the way they should. But then, maybe they had. He was just talking about making the guy's work schedule. Mason was his boss. Plus, Gavin obviously had a whole lot of shit going on in his life right now. Fucking his boss might not be something he wanted to deal with.

"Yeah...maybe. Still wish I could have sucked you off before we decided that."

Gavin laughed, his hand on the door as he stood there. "You're not the only one who wishes that."

Mason smiled at him. "Have a good day, Teach. Go in there and jack off while you think about me."

Gavin's brow kicked up. "That an order, boss?"

"It sure is."

They said their goodbyes and Mason drove off. When he got home he did exactly what he told Gavin to do—rubbed one out thinking about Gavin. Then, he sat in bed naked to figure out the work schedule.

Every shift Gavin worked, he worked with Mason.

***

It was Tuesday. Gavin hadn't seen Mason since their day out on Sunday. He would be working Wednesday, Friday and Saturday this week, and he pretty much had nothing going on until he went in for his first day tomorrow.

I should go see my parents... It wasn't the first time he thought that the past couple days, yet still he didn't go—just continued letting his fingers strum his guitar.

Bang, bang, bang, bang! A loud thump came through the front door before, "Let me in, you hermit!"

As he stood, Gavin set his guitar down and rolled his eyes at Braden. As soon as he opened the door, his loud-mouthed friend started speaking again. "You move to Blackcreek because you missed me so much, yet I haven't seen you since the wedding. What's been going on?"

"Back porch?" Gavin asked.

"Sure."

They headed out and sat down. "I didn't move here because I missed you."

"Sure you did. So what's been going on with you?"

"Not a lot. I got a job."

"No shit?" Braden put his feet up on the porch railing. "That was quick. I figured the process would take more time getting hired at a school."

Gavin made it a point not to look at Braden when he replied. "I'm not working at a school." He wasn't sure how he felt about that, either.

"Teaching at a music store or something?"

Still no eye contact. If he did, Braden would push harder. His friend already didn't know when to quit. "Nope. I'm a bartender."

He felt Braden's eyes on him.

"I don't want to talk about it. I just...don't know what I want to do." And that was the truth.

"Fine. Fair enough. Can we talk about the bite mark on your neck?" Braden jammed his finger into the tender spot by Gavin's throat. "Looks like you move a lot quicker than you used to. Good for you."

Gavin shoved him. "Fuck you." When Braden sat there watching him, Gavin knew he had no choice but to continue. *This* Braden wouldn't let go. "It's nothing. It was Mason. Considering he's my boss, it's probably better that we got interrupted before much of anything could start." He wasn't sure why he didn't share more about their day—the skydiving and the hike. Gavin wanted to keep that to himself.

"No, actually, it's not better that way. I assure you, getting off is always the better alternative to not getting off. Do you like him?"

What were they, twelve? "I don't know him. He's sexy, so there's a part of me that likes him." Gavin winked at Braden. "He's a cool guy to be around." He got Gavin to go skydiving with him. He wasn't sure he would have done that with anyone else, yet it had been an easy yes with Mason. "I enjoy his company, but—"

"But nothing. You've always been like this. You just let life pass you by. You don't really go after anything. You're always tightening your own reigns. If you like him, go after him. If you don't know, at least get laid. Have some fun, Gav. Live your life. You deserve it. There's nothing wrong with who you are."

"I know that." And he did. He didn't know what held him back more often than not. Why he was willing to let life pass him by and keep himself in the shadows.

"Preventing yourself from enjoying your life isn't going to make them change their minds. This is a new start. Let yourself have it. Or at least let Mason fuck your brains out. Jesus Christ, I'll hire you a male escort if I have to."

"I'm not that hard up. I don't have to pay for it." Gavin chuckled but didn't really feel it.

"Hey," Braden said, more seriously this time. "You've done everything right in your life. You've been a great son, a good friend to me, and you were a good first boyfriend, too. You've sacrificed enough, don't you think? Isn't it about time to find out who Gavin Davis really is?"

Yes. "And I'll learn that by letting Mason fuck my brains out?"

"Maybe. Maybe not. I'm sure you'll have a whole lot of fun regardless."

With that, Braden pushed to his feet and said his goodbyes. Gavin didn't move from his spot on the porch.

Chapter Nine

Tuesdays were never really busy, but tonight had been crazy. After turning off the open sign and locking the door, Mason didn't feel like doing anything. Instead of straddling a barstool and opening a bottle, like he wanted to, he went into the kitchen to check on the back. "Everything okay, Dana?"

"Yep. Dishes are done. The kitchen is all cleaned up, except for whatever you have left out front. I'll help you out there real quick."

Mason waved her off. "No, that's okay. I'll finish up and close up. You can head on out." Despite being exhausted, if Mason could do things himself, he always preferred that.

"Are you sure?" The blonde asked. She was a college student who lived in her parent's old house in Blackcreek but drove into the city for school. She had to be even more tired than Mason.

"No, really. I got it. You can go."

"Thanks. My feet are killing me and I still have an essay to finish." It was after midnight, so that didn't look real good for her.

"No problem. Keep up the good work. I'll see you soon."

She grabbed her things and then headed for the door. Mason walked her to her car like he always did. When she pulled off he heard, "Mind if I come in?" from behind him. He didn't have to turn to know the sleep-roughed voice belonged to Gavin.

Mason headed his way. "Yeah, sure. You sound like you sleep-drove here." He locked the door behind them both, and went for the bar. "You want a drink?"

"Jack and coke." Gavin sat on a stool while Mason made him a drink. Gavin ran a hand through his hair that was messier than it usually was. He seemed frazzled, jittery.

"Everything okay?"

"I talked to Braden."

"Always a scary thing."

Gavin laughed, then took a drink. "I couldn't sleep tonight. My mind kept going and going. I couldn't turn the damn thing off."

He wasn't sure why, but Mason had a feeling he'd need a drink too so he poured himself one. "What has your mind runnin', teach?"

"My parents. Myself. Life. You. Sex."

Mason particularly liked the last two.

Gavin swallowed down everything in his glass before tapping it for a refill. "Did you know I've only been with three men after Braden? And none of them more than a couple times each."

Mason's throat burned and he coughed, almost choking on his Jack.

"That sounds like a tragedy to me."

"When my parents found out I was gay—porn of course—they lost it. Tears, broken hearts, family meetings with people from the church, the whole nine. I decided I could pretend—for them I would. Or maybe I really did think I could change it. Then I met Braden and he just sort of...woke me up. He's good at that, like a damned tornado storming into your life. We dated, went to *prom*, and I broke my parents' hearts again by being true to who I am. It's a lot of weight to carry, trying to keep your soul from burning for eternity for your parents."

He sighed. "Anyway, we moved away after high school. I think he did it for me. Mom got depressed and started seeing a shrink."

Mason leaned on the bar. "Did you love him? Braden?"

"Nah. Thought I did for a bit. He saved me back then, though. I wasn't...things weren't good for me up here." He tapped his head. "Not in here, either." Then his chest. "I think that's why I wanted to help that kid. I saw myself in him. I hadn't had anyone to help me until Braden, and I didn't want that boy to suffer the same way."

Some of the tension on Mason's chest drifted off. "You're a good guy."

Gavin shrugged. He didn't look convinced. "Anyway, I was never real good at—I don't know, going for what I wanted? When Braden left I let myself get wrapped up in finishing college. From there I got wrapped up in work. Before I knew it, I realized I hadn't had anyone in my life for years."

Gavin finished his second drink. When he tapped it again, Mason took the glass away. That wasn't what he needed tonight. "Sounds like a lonely life."

"No." Gavin shook his head. "That's the thing. I was happy. Or I thought I was. I love music. I was good at what I did. I had friends and spent time with colleagues. It's not as though I kept inside myself."

Those words put the weight right back on Mason's chest. Gavin clearly didn't see. "But you did, in some ways. You kept yourself alone. You let yourself get wrapped up in work and other people's lives so you didn't have to deal with your sexuality."

"No." Gavin stood, and started pacing the bar. "I've never really doubted who I am. I was with men. I never dated women. I might not have been completely open with it, but I know I'm gay. My family knows I'm gay."

"Because you fucked some random guy once or twice a year? That doesn't mean you had a love life. Hell, it's not even a sex life—not a good one, at least. You wanted to pretend that part of you didn't exist so you wouldn't let your family down. You wanted to be a teacher the way they were because then you wouldn't feel like you let them down. Wanting a man doesn't mean you let someone down, Teach." Mason knew he was probably way out of line, but right now, he didn't give a shit. He walked over to Gavin and grabbed his arm so the man stopped moving. "What kind of life is it if you're not living your own?"

**

He'd hardly known Mason any time at all. Yes, they spent a lot of time talking the day they went hiking, but somehow, Mason just summed up Gavin better than anyone in his life ever could, except maybe Braden. It had taken Braden a whole hell of a lot longer to get to know him than it did Mason.

And he thought he understood Mason pretty well himself. Maybe it was so easy for Mason to see Gavin because the two men were so much alike. "Are we talking about you or me?"

Mason's hold on his arm briefly tightened before he let go completely. "Good call. Both of us, and you know it. That's why I bought this bar, remember? To live my own life."

Though, Gavin knew Mason hadn't planned to stay. He'd bought it as an experiment before going right back to the restaurants and Denver.

It was crazy how alike they were in some ways, yet so different. Gavin's whole life, he'd wanted parents who one hundred percent accepted him the way he was. If he had that, everything else would fall into place. Here Mason had grown up having just what Gavin wanted, yet it seemed he felt pressure, too. He'd still felt the need to be something specific for his family.

He watched as Mason walked over to a chair, turned it backward and sat down. Gavin didn't know why he got a kick out of the fact that Mason always sat in a chair, straddling the back. It made his pants ride up, outlining the bulge between his legs. Gavin started to go hard behind his fly.

"And that's why I'm here." Gavin sat across from Mason at the table. The man raised a brow at him. He did that a lot.

"Here in Blackcreek or here in my bar?"

Gavin wasn't used to making his needs known. Not really. Braden had approached him, and then as they got older, when he wanted a man he went to a bar and waited for someone to approach him.

He was so damned tired of taking a backseat in his own life. "Both. I came to Blackcreek for a fresh start. I'm at your bar because I want you to fuck me." When Mason didn't continue he added, "We're attracted to each other. I see the way you look at me. I felt what I do to you when we went hiking. Between you and me, the work thing doesn't matter. I'm tired of not taking what I want."

The silence stretched on and he started to sweat. Hell, was Mason going to turn him down? He put himself out there, offered himself to the guy, and he had nothing to say?

Gavin moved to stand but Mason grabbed his arm again, holding him in place. "Are you sure about that? It's important we get things out there, because I *am* your employer. Whether we have sex or not, it will never affect your job. We're two grown men. I think we can handle that."

"I agree," Gavin replied.

"I want you. Make no mistake about that. But there's one more thing we have to discuss. You said you want me to fuck you. I don't do the fucking."

Holy shit. He hadn't expected that one. "Ever?"

"I've done it, more than once. It's not something I have a real interest in. I want to *be* fucked." He leaned forward, giving Gavin a whiff of his spicy scent. "That doesn't mean I won't take control. I'll want you inside me when I tell you to be there. I'll want you to kiss me and suck me and touch me when I tell you to, but it will be your cock in my ass. That going to be a problem for you?"

Lust shot through him, landing straight in his crotch. Gavin's half-hard dick went painfully erect. He'd almost always bottomed. Not because it was a preference as much as how things always happened to go down.

He wanted what Mason just laid out for him, though.

Wanted it so bad he feared the second he pushed inside Mason, he'd lose it. "No. Definitely not a problem."

Mason stood and nodded toward the back. "Let's go, then."

Chapter Ten

Mason led Gavin to his office.

"I'm clean, just so you know. I get tested once a year to be safe. The last time was about a month before I moved here. I haven't been with anyone since. I have the results at home, not as though that helps us now, but—"

Mason felt an amused smile spread across his face. "You're rambling. Do I make you nervous?"

"You make me horny," Gavin replied.

"Nervous and horny?" Mason opened the door for Gavin to go inside.

He stopped in front of Mason and said flatly, "Annoyed and horny," before continuing to go inside.

Ah, so Gavin didn't like to be called out on his nerves. Mason barked out a laugh. "As long as there's a horny in there, we're good. And for what it's worth, I'm clean as well. I was in a long term, committed relationship until a couple months ago. We still both were checked regularly, and my last results are recent as well. We'll still use condoms for now, though."

Mason grabbed a rubber and lube from his desk drawer. When he reached Gavin again, the right side of Gavin's mouth kicked up. "That's handy."

"Always be prepared." He tossed them onto the couch and then grabbed Gavin's hand, making him cup Mason's bulge. "See what you do to me? Even that first day when you came in telling me I'm shit at the guitar, you got me hard."

"I'll give you lessons." Gavin squeezed, rubbing the palm of his hand against Mason. He had a good grip. Mason's body buzzed. Yeah, he definitely wanted this.

"Now's when I'm gonna want you to kiss me, Teach."

And Gavin did. His mouth came down fast and hard on Mason's. Their tongues battled, each wanting to possess, to control. Mason tasted liquor on Gavin's tongue. He smelled faintly of fresh wood.

He liked it. He wanted to smell sweat on him next. Sweat and come.

"Get undressed and sit on the couch. I'm going to suck you, and then ride you. Don't come too early or you'll fuck it up for both of us."

"Fuck…" Gavin struggled to rip his shirt over his head. When he did it dropped to the floor. His pants came next, then the black briefs were gone and his prick sprung free. Long and thick, with pulsing veins running the length, nestled in a patch of dark hair, just the way Mason liked.

He grabbed Gavin's erection and squeezed. "You're gonna fill me up nice."

Gavin's body tensed. He groaned out every curse in the book before pulling at Mason's shirt. "You're going to want to hurry."

Again, he made Mason laugh. "Eager?"

"Dying."

Yeah, Mason was, too. Not just to get laid, either, but to get laid by Gavin. He was so fresh, wide-eyed and innocent, without being naïve. Everything seemed like a new experience for him, and for some reason that really did something to Mason.

He let Gavin take off his shirt, then took care of his own jeans. "Sit."

"You're gorgeous." Gavin ran a hand down Mason's abs.

"Thanks. So are you. Now sit down so I can put your dick in my mouth."

***

Gavin wasn't going to make Mason tell him again. His knees cracked as he sat down on the couch. Mason went down, too, kneeling in front of him.

"Tell me before you come." And then his tongue swirled around the swollen head of Gavin's erection. Gavin jerked, a bolt of electricity ripping through him.

Mason kept licking. He didn't take Gavin deep. Not yet. He just sucked the head—licked and sucked, like he had all the time in the world.

Every once in a while, he probed the hole, and when he did Gavin felt like he could rip out of his skin, the need to come was so strong.

The teasing was torture, and right before Gavin moved his hand, ready to grab Mason's head and pull him farther down, he leaned forward.

"Fuck."

"What?" Gavin asked.

"I told you I liked to be fucked, so do it."

That was all the incentive Gavin needed. He tightened his hands in Mason's hair and did what Mason said. Gavin fucked.

He pumped his hips upward. Each time he did, his cock hit the back of Mason's throat and he swallowed, deep-throating Gavin in a way no one ever had.

The suction was just right, Mason's mouth warm and wet and to-die-for. Gavin wanted to come down the back of his throat. Wanted to release, but he fought off the urge building inside him.

He thrust harder when Mason palmed his balls, tugging them a little. This time he could tell Mason almost gagged, but it didn't make the man pull off of Gavin.

It was that that made the pressure too much. Made his balls tighten. Made his cock want to spill. "That's it… fuck, that's it. If you don't stop I'm going to lose it."

And then Mason's mouth was gone. He nodded toward the condom. "Put it on."

Gavin almost didn't do it just because Mason told him to, but decided he liked the way the man controlled things when it came to sex. He ripped the package open and started to cover himself. The break gave his body exactly what he needed to get himself under control again.

Mason went for the lube, coating his fingers and then reaching behind himself as he still kneeled between Gavin's legs. "Oh, hell." That was quite possibly one of the sexiest things he'd ever seen—watching Mason lube and prep his own asshole for Gavin.

Mason winked at him. "You can do it next time."

"But then I can't watch you do it. Next time I want a better view."

There went that damn brow again. "Maybe."

After he lubed his hole, Mason slicked up Gavin's prick. Even the simple touch almost sent him over the edge. He wanted inside Mason and he wanted there now.

"Sit on my lap."

"Not your call."

Gavin caught his eye, thought, and then said, "Will you sit on me?"

Mason nodded and then climbed onto Gavin. He straddled him, weight on his knees and shins. Leaning forward, he used one hand to tilt Gavin's head up. When he did, Mason kissed him. It was a battle, yet not. Rough and hungry, yet Gavin let Mason lead the way.

Tongues tangled and teeth clashed. Gavin's body buzzed when Mason pulled up a little higher, when he grabbed Gavin's dick and lined it up with his asshole.

In this moment he was pretty sure he'd follow wherever Mason led him. He guided the whole way, slowing helping Gavin push his way past the tight pucker. It took a minute and some finagling before his head pushed inside.

"Oh, fuck." It was a tight grip on the crown of his cock. Mason didn't slow down, though. He pushed down, letting Gavin slide into him inch by inch.

They both cursed when Gavin was all the way inside, Mason's ass on his thighs. "This is where you're going to want to jerk me off, Teach." The second the words left Mason's mouth, he rose up and sat again.

Motherfucker, this felt good. "Yeah, boss. I'm on it." He wrapped a hand around Mason's thick erection and pumped. As he did Mason moved on him, up and down, riding Gavin the way he said he would.

Gavin's dick sang Mason's praises as his hole squeezed it. His skin felt hot, fiery. Hell, he was burning up from the inside out.

He jerked harder, faster.

"Tighter," Mason told him, and he did. He gripped harder. "That's it. Fuck yeah, that's it. Fuck me harder, too."

Gavin's vision went blurry. It was almost like he was possessed as he let loose on Mason, thrusting hard, up and into him.

His balls hurt. The orgasm was right there. Had been for a while now. "I'm not going to last much longer."

"Then make me come." Mason kept moving. Gavin, too. He kept hold of Mason's cock, kept working him. Kept fucking him. Mason's hand went to Gavin's neck, to the spot he'd bitten Gavin while on the hike.

Gavin suddenly wanted to mark Mason as well. He leaned forward, teeth into Mason's pec, and bit down. Sticky liquid shot up between them, ran down his hand. Spurt after spurt, Mason's semen landed on them both, just as Gavin shot, too. Filling the condom as he kept pumping in Mason's ass.

"I'm going to die." He dropped his head backward against the couch when he'd been rung dry. Yet at the same time he felt…weightless. Free. Invincible. Fan-fucking-tastic. "Please tell me you're going to let me do that again."

Chapter Eleven

"If you're good." Mason winked at Gavin and stood. He pulled the condom off his lover and tossed it in the trashcan. Who was he kidding, though? He'd definitely let Gavin fuck him again. They were both single. The guy was sexy and good in the sack. He didn't know Gavin real well, but he liked what he saw. Mason liked *him,* and they had a good time together.

"Do you have a towel or something so we can clean off?" Gavin asked.

Mason walked over and sat beside him. "Nope. Good sex is messy sex. Leave it."

"And we'll also be fucking again. You said if I'm good, and that was better than good."

Yeah, it was. "Greedy, aren't you?" Mason reached over and rubbed his spunk into Gavin's chest, loving the feel of the coarse hair there. "Tell me more about your job and how all that shit went down."

Before Mason had all the words out, Gavin already began shaking his head. "Not right now. It'll put me in a bad mood, and I don't want to be in one right now."

He liked that about Gavin—he was a man who told the truth. He didn't blow off the question or divert. He said exactly why he didn't want to answer it at this time. "Fair enough."

"What about you? Would your parents really have been so upset if you opened a bar earlier?"

Mason let his head roll to the side so he could look at Gavin. What a sight they probably made—two naked men, sprawled out on a couch, discussing life. "Yes and no. It's all about expectation. I know you understand that part of it. They loved me with all they had. They wanted the best for me. They wanted to pass down their lifetime of hard work to me. I'm an only child. As far as I knew, my parents tried for years to have a baby and they finally had me. They tried for years after I was born and never had any more. Of course now I see that's because I was never really theirs—"

"Yeah, you are," Gavin interrupted.

Mason let his eyes fall closed, frustrated. "You're right. I shouldn't have said that. They've always been my parents." They would do anything for Mason. That's why walking away from their dream for him had always been so hard, despite his need to build something on his own. He'd thought he could handle working on Creekside and then either selling it or hiring someone to run it for him, but that wasn't the truth. Now, he couldn't imagine walking away. Even for them. He loved them, so it felt like a betrayal not to want Alexander's.

Because they were his parents. He was back at that. He was lucky to have the family he did.

He flinched when he felt Gavin's thumb on his forehead. "You're deep in thought. Your forehead is wrinkled."

"Maybe if you straighten them out for me, the thoughts won't be there anymore." He wanted them gone. Thought maybe Gavin might have it in him to wipe Mason's worry away—or at least to make him forget about it for a while.

"Do you feel that way? Like you're not theirs? That's bullshit, you know."

Mason opened his eyes. "I appreciate the effort, but this is way too heavy a conversation when I'm still rung out from blowing my load."

"You started it," Gavin countered.

He did, but, "Now, I'm ending it."

Gavin sighed. "Fair enough." He returned Mason's words from a few minutes before. "I should go. I have to be up early. I'm going out to see my parents for a couple hours before work tomorrow night." Gavin stood, grabbed his underwear and pulled them on while Mason enjoyed the view.

"You have a nice ass."

"But you don't like to fuck?"

"I love ass. I just want a dick in mine. I'll eat yours sometime, though."

"If you're good." Gavin grabbed his pants next.

Mason chuckled. "Touché."

Once Gavin was dressed, Mason took the time to do the same thing.

Gavin helped him finish up the last few things he needed to do to close the bar down and then they both headed to the cars, which were parked by one another.

Mason held Gavin's face and covered Gavin's mouth with his own. He nipped Gavin's lip with his teeth and explored Gavin's mouth with his tongue. When his cock started to go hard again, he pulled back. "I love kissing. Kissing and fucking. I could do them all day long. It sounds like the perfect day—doing nothing but sleeping, kissing and fucking. I've always kept too busy for that, though."

"Yeah, me, too."

Mason watched as Gavin got into his car before getting into his own. They left at the same time, two sets of lights until at one point, he went left and Gavin went right. The whole time he couldn't stop thinking about Gavin's question. Did he feel like he didn't belong in his family anymore?

The truth was, he didn't know.

***

"Who are you again?" Gavin's dad looked over at his mom, lost. His hair was all grey, though it had been mostly grey for a while now. He looked more fragile than he used to. His father sat in a twin bed with plain, white sheets. The room wasn't decorated much, and what was there didn't all belong to him. Some things, yes. To keep things familiar, he assumed, but the shelves and tables and bed... None of it was his father's.

A nursing home. It's not something he ever really thought about before his dad got sick. As weak as it made him, it was something he wished he didn't have to see.

"I'm your wife, remember?" His mom's hand shook as she held a picture of the two of them together. "We've been married nearly fifty years."

Gavin's parents hadn't had him until they were in their forties. It used to embarrass him when he was younger—the fact that his parents were so much older than everyone else's.

"And who is this?" Gavin's gut twisted into knots when his dad pointed at him. His father didn't know him. He'd stayed away for too long, and now it was too late.

"He's Gavin, our son."

His father stared at him, no recollection on his face. "I have a son?" His voice now even softer. Gavin rubbed his finger across the seam of his jeans, pretending it was the strings on his guitar.

"Hey, Dad. How are you doing?"

His father didn't answer, turning to look at his mom again. He opened and closed his mouth but nothing came out.

"He's a good boy, Edward. He's a teacher like we were. He works at a real good school. We're very proud of him."

Only they weren't, were they? Not if those reasons she just mentioned were what they had to be proud of. Gavin worked at a bar now. He'd lost his job for trying to help a gay kid that his parents would think was going to Hell like their son.

His mom reached for his dad but the man shook his head. He got fidgety, obviously unsure and frustrated. She reached for him again but his father shoved her hand away. He never would have done that before.

"Is there any other family I have that I don't know about? More kids? Grandchildren? Are you hiding my family from me?" He faced Gavin, anger sparking off his words. "Do you have a wife and kids I should know about? Why are you hiding my family from me?" And then he was silent a beat before, "We always wanted a big family, didn't we? I think I remember that. Did Gavin give us that? Grandkids?" *That* was his father, not the angry man he'd seen a second ago, and he still wanted the things he'd always wanted.

A heavy weight landed in Gavin's chest, as though someone stood on it. His mom's face paled. He raised a hand to her mouth, the limb shaking. So now he not only had parents who feared for his soul, he had to feel guilty for not giving his father the family he wanted while the man was slowly losing his mind.

"No, no family yet, Dad." Likely not ever, and not just because he was gay. Gavin just wasn't sure he ever wanted kids. Maybe, maybe not. A husband, yes. Sharing his life with someone he loved the way Braden did with Wes, he wanted that. He hadn't decided on the rest of it, though.

That's where his mom jumped in. "I have no doubt it will happen soon. He's such a handsome, responsible man. Any woman would feel honored to be married to Gavin."

Fire burned through his veins at his mom's words. He spent most of his life, not completely in the closet, but keeping who he was under wraps. He'd just decided he wasn't doing that any longer, and now with that one statement she asked him to do it again. "Mom."

Her eyes got glassy, a plea inside them, lassoing Gavin, pulling him in. *Shit.* He opened his mouth to break her heart, the way he'd done so much in the past, when his father started speaking again. "That's good. I'm so proud of you, son. Now tell me about the school you teach at."

Chapter Twelve

Mason groaned when he heard the familiar creak of the front door and looked up to see Isaac walk in. They were busy for a Wednesday night, and Gavin had texted to let Mason know he would be a little late. The last thing he needed to deal with tonight was his ex.

Isaac's voice rose above the crowd. "You need to get that door fixed! I can do it for you." He sat in the only empty bar stool. What the hell was it with tonight? They shouldn't be this busy.

"I can fix it myself. I just haven't had the time. What the hell are you doing here?" Mason cleared some of the glasses off the bar.

"I'm coming to see my oldest friend at his bar."

Shit. Isaac was right about that. They'd been friends their whole life, and then lovers. Still… "The friend you lied to?"

Isaac cursed. "I didn't lie. It wasn't my place to tell you, Mase." He had a sincerity in his eyes that Mason didn't want to see there. He wanted to be angry.

"This was a good investment. You'll have to hire someone who really knows what they're doing when you come back to Denver."

And that ended the break in his anger for his ex. "Isaac—"

"Excuse me. Can I get another beer?" a man asked from the other end of the counter.

"Shit. I'll be right back."

"Looks like you need some help in this place, no? It would be the perfect time to train someone."

Mason shook his head. "I have help. He's just running late." Mason filled multiple beer glasses, made a mixed drink, and then took money before he looked up and saw Gavin walk in.

He looked worn out as hell, his hair messy like he'd spent the day in bed fucking. Mason headed the other way again, meeting Gavin behind the bar, not a foot away from Isaac.

"Sorry I'm late. I know that doesn't put me off to the best start. I just…some shit went down today."

Mason gabbed his bicep and squeezed before pulling his hand away. "Nah, it's cool. Everyone and their brother just decided to come in tonight."

"Excuse me, can I get a drink?" Isaac asked. Mason turned to tell him to fuck off when Gavin said, "What can I get you?" at the same time as someone held up an empty pitcher from one of the tables by the stage.

"He'll want whiskey, on the rocks. I'll be right back." Busy or not, he didn't want to leave his customers waiting. Plus, the more pitchers he filled, the more money the bar made.

Mason made rounds, refreshing drinks where need be. Gavin kept busy behind the bar. Mason could see he looked a little frazzled but he held his own, so Mason kept clear. He knew it would be important to the man to be able to hold his weight, and the only way to let that happen was not to rescue him unless he needed it.

He visited with some of the patrons while taking orders.

"Excuse me, I seem to be having some trouble with the jukebox," a redhead woman said to him.

"I'll give you a hand." Mason walked over with her. "Sometimes you have to rough it up to get it to cooperate." He shook it, and after he did, a song started to play.

"Thank you," she gave him a seductive smile before leaning against the wall. "What's your name?"

"Mason. I own the place."

"Oh, wow. It's a great bar. I'm Melody." Another smile.

Shit.

"Mason, I've been looking for you all over," Isaac stepped up beside him. Mason took this as the opportunity to let her know that unfortunately, he wouldn't be interested in her.

"Nice to meet you, Melody. This is my ex Isaac." It was the easiest way he could think of to let her know that he wasn't interested.

"Oh, well don't I feel stupid." She blushed. "All the good looking ones are gay." She winked at them and walked away.

Isaac laughed. "Why are you always getting yourself into trouble with women?"

"Hell if I know." But it was true. Mason spent a lot of time getting hit on by women. Isaac had saved him more than once in the past. But the truth was, even though he wasn't attracted to women, he loved them. Some of the most important people in his life had been women. "Guess I'm just sexier than you." They both laughed this time. Mason glanced up to see Gavin look at him. He pulled on the lobe of his right ear. Hmm, he usually only did that when he was nervous. Mason winked at him.

"Who's the guy?" Isaac asked.

"My bartender."

Isaac crossed his arms. "Is he fucking you?"

He heard the competitiveness in Isaac's voice. Mason didn't think for a second it was because Isaac was broken hearted or couldn't handle the thought of Mason with another man. Again, it all came down to winning with his ex.

"Maybe, maybe not." Mason grinned at Isaac and then went for the bar.

***

Gavin watched as Mason ambled through the bar. The other man stood with his arms crossed, watching him go. And very obviously enjoying the view. Not that he could blame him. Mason was an attractive man...an attractive man who had known what drink his friend would want. Someone he obviously felt very comfortable with, though Gavin had a feeling Mason would be that way with close to anyone.

"Excuse me, can I get another?" A blonde woman asked him. Shit, he needed to get it together.

Gavin stepped over and started another cosmo. He poured in the Vodka and triple sec before grabbing a straw. As he went to hand it to her a voice said, "You forgot the cranberry juice. It's a kamikaze without it."

Damn it. He really needed to get his head in the game. A cosmo was one of the easiest drinks there was, but he left his head back with his parents. "Been a long day."

"We didn't get to be properly introduced. I'm Isaac, Mason's ex-boyfriend and best friend from when he was a child."

"One of my best friends, but I'm reconsidering. You're being a dickhead, Isaac. No one is playing a game here except for you."

"What?" He held up his hands to Mason as if in surrender. "I'm just introducing myself to your help."

White, hot anger exploded inside Gavin. His hand fisted on the glass. He wasn't a violent man. Hell, he was pretty easy going, but after the day he had, he wasn't in the mood to take shit from anyone. Lowering his voice, Gavin stepped closer. "I'm a little more than the help considering where I spent last night."

As soon as the words left his mouth he wanted them back. Yeah, he'd fucked Mason, but that had been all it was. He didn't have any claim on the man, and definitely didn't have the right to be jealous right now.

"Hey, you okay?" Mason asked, concern in his voice.

No, he really wasn't. *It's the end of his life, Gavin. Give him some peace. Don't break his heart again. Don't make him go, fearing for his son…*

"Is that supposed to matter? Ask me how many nights I've spent with him." Isaac didn't back down. The urge to say something else hit Gavin but he bit it back. Mason wasn't his. Hell, he didn't know him well enough to want him as his. So, he did what he did best. Kept his mouth shut.

Mason grabbed the cosmo out of his hand and handed it to the waiting woman, who no doubt heard their whole conversation. "On the house, sweetheart." Mason winked at her. She took the drink and walked away.

He poured whisky in a glass and handed it over to Isaac next. "Go sit down at one of the tables."

"Are you dismissing me?" Isaac grinned cockily.

"I'm going to kick your ass in a second. Christ, you're being an asshole on purpose. Go sit down before I make you leave."

"You always did like being in control." Isaac winked at Mason, took the drink, and then left for one of the tables.

"Your ex is a charming man." Gavin made a trip up and down the bar to see if anyone needed a drink. A large group of people had left, so they weren't quite as busy as they had been.

"He's used to getting his way, and he likes to rile shit up. It's just the way it is. I'm more concerned about you, because you avoid confrontation, yet you didn't back there."

Was that a nice way for Mason to say he thought Gavin was weak? "How do you know what I avoid and what I don't?"

Mason cocked that damn brow at him again. It pissed Gavin off that he thought it was sexy. He wanted to be angry right now. He needed to be.

"What's wrong, man?" Mason asked again. Damned if Gavin didn't want to tell him. If he didn't want to share with someone how angry he was. How hurt…

"Can we get a drink?" someone called.

Mason held up a hand, "Just a second."

"We're at work. That's what we need to be doing—working."

"Gavin." Mason grabbed his arm. Isaac was right. He did like control.

"I had a bad day. I got a flat tire, and had some shit to deal with. That's all. Can I do my job now?"

Lucky for him, that answer seemed to satisfy Mason. "That's all you had to say, teach."

"And deprive you of the opportunity to push? I'd never do that, boss."

"That's what I want to hear." Mason smiled at him, and then the two of them went back to work. Gavin's mood didn't improve but he did a good job at hiding it.

Isaac stayed until closing. Once the bar emptied, Gavin saw him talking with Mason, before he headed toward the bathroom and Mason headed over to Gavin.

He leaned against the counter and crossed his arm. "He's too drunk to drive. I have to take him home with me."

A vein pulsed in the side of Gavin's forehead. "Makes sense." He moved down the bar, continuing to wipe it down.

"Hey." Somehow, that one word from Mason had the power to stop Gavin.

"What?"

"It's complicated with Isaac, but we're over."

Some of the tension deflated from Gavin's body, which then annoyed him. He shouldn't care. They'd screwed. The end. "You don't owe me anything."

"I'm telling you all the same."

Gavin nodded, more grateful than he should feel. "Okay, then."

He turned to finish up his job when another, "Hey," from Mason stopped him.

Gavin looked at him, and then Mason spoke, low and with authority. "Now's gonna be another one of those times you want to kiss me."

Stepping closer to him, Gavin did as Mason said.

Chapter Thirteen

"Did you really have to make me sleep on the couch last night?" Isaac asked while Mason poured himself a cup of coffee. "My neck is killing me, though I guess it makes sense. It always was hard for you to keep your hands off me."

He leaned back and blew into his mug before taking a drink. Isaac wanted a big response and Mason wouldn't give him one. "I have a few things to take care of before I go to work. I'll drop you off so you can get your car first."

Isaac ran a hand through his dark hair, obviously having expected Mason to say something else. "The guy at the bar…what's he do?"

"He's a bartender."

Isaac scoffed. "He may be working as a bartender right now but it's not what he does, just like it's not what you do."

It was now. That was the difference between Mason and Isaac; one of the differences, at least. Isaac could never be happy at something like tending a bar, whether he owned it or not. Not unless that bar was a chain all over the state or the US. "He's a music teacher. Why are you so interested in him?"

Isaac ignored that. "Are you really letting him fuck you?"

What he really meant by that question was, are you letting him fuck you and not me? "Do you need a shower?"

"With you?"

Mason sighed. "You're coming off as desperate. That's not like you." Mason took another drink and then stood. "I'm going to take a shower."

As soon as the words left his mouth, Isaac's phone rang. He pulled it out of his pocket. The smile on Isaac's face told Mason everything he needed to know. "Don't answer it."

He swiped the screen. "Hello, Mom. How are you?"

And by Mom, he meant Mason's mother. "Shit," he mumbled.

"That's good. I'm doing well. Just sitting here having a cup of coffee with Mason."

Motherfucker. Mason would kill him.

"Yeah, sure, you can talk to him."

Isaac held the phone out to him, and Mason shook his head. This wasn't okay. Not at all. When he didn't take it right away, Isaac covered it with his hand, his voice soft when he said, "she's still your mom, Mase."

He knew that. He did...but why couldn't he feel it? Not that Mason loved his parents any less, but things felt different now. Could they really love him the way he always thought they had? His whole life felt like a lie now.

Mason reached out and took the phone from him. "Hey, Mom."

"Hello. How are you?" He hated the tentativeness in her voice, though did he expect anything different? He'd been standoffish. He wasn't proud of that, but it was true.

"I'm doing well. I've been keeping busy." His way of excusing the fact that he rarely called.

"How is the bar going?"

"Really well. We stay pretty steady most nights. Just like the restaurants, the weekends are the busiest. I recently had to hire a new bartender."

"Oh, wow. That's great, Mason. It sounds like things are going wonderfully. We sure miss you around here. Not just the family, but people ask about you all the time. You've always been like that. Everyone loves you."

Guilt created a vacuum inside him, sucking out all his air. Regardless of blood, this was the woman who raised him. The woman who took care of him and loved him. She was also the woman who lied to him his whole life. Why couldn't he forget that?

"I miss you guys, too. I'll come visit soon. It's just so hard with the bar."

"Of course… we understand. Though, we can always come there as well. We'd love to see the place. I see you have Isaac out."

No, he hadn't had Isaac out at all. The man had just shown up. There was a difference, and that's exactly where he'd feared this conversation would go. One of the places, at least.

"He's one of my oldest friends, Mom. That's all."

She sighed. "I just feel so guilty. It wasn't Isaac's fault. He hadn't known for long, and he didn't tell you because we asked him not to. You grew up with him. You two were happy together. I hate to see you throw that away because of our mistake."

How did he tell his mom that wasn't it? That they were friends and had great sex and staying together had been easy, more than anything? They knew what each other liked and didn't have to worry about the other getting upset when they spent too much time at work. Mason didn't want the same things anymore.

"He misses you," his mom added.

Mason tried not to get frustrated. "I know you mean well, but I'm too old to have my mother play matchmaker. I'm a big boy, and so is Isaac. People break up all the time."

"I know that. I just…"

She didn't have to finish for him to know what she meant. She felt bad and she wanted to make up for it. Trying to get him back together with Isaac couldn't do that, though. Hell, he wasn't even sure if she had something to make up for. Mason just didn't know what he felt anymore. "I get it, Mom. Listen, I hate to cut this short but I have to go. I'll call soon, okay? And I'll make it back home."

"Okay…bye, Mason. We love you."

"I love you, too." Mason hung up the phone and stared at Isaac with hard eyes. "Don't bring them into this game you're playing, Isaac.

You're going to hurt them."

He shrugged. "Maybe it's not a game."

Mason didn't have time for this. Shaking his head, he went to the bathroom to take a shower and try to forget about his ex and their morning.

***

"We're going to start with middle "C" and finger warm-ups. This key is middle "C"." Gavin pressed down and watched Jessie smile. "Here, put your right hand on the keys like this." He showed her, and Jessie did as he asked. "Start with your thumb and then press each finger down on the key it rests on."

Gavin worked on the piano with Jessie for an hour before she looked up at him and asked him to play a song for her.

"What do you want to hear?"

She thought for a second. "Something fun." When she looked at him with her big eyes, he suddenly felt a hundred pounds of pressure weighing him down. He didn't want to let her down. He glanced over at Wes and Braden, who sat at the kitchen table.

Gavin didn't even have to speak for Braden to say, "See what we deal with? It's impossible not to want to give her the world."

Yeah, he definitely saw it.

"Thank you," Jessie grinned happily.

Oh boy. They were in trouble with her. Gavin turned toward the piano again and just let himself play. He chose Fur Elise. He wasn't sure if Jessie would consider it fun but most people seemed to like it. It's always what students asked to learn.

Gavin's heart beat along with the notes of the song. His body felt in tune to it the way he always did when he played.

When he moved to Blackcreek, he'd had to sell his piano. Though it hadn't been long, he missed it. He didn't realize how much until he started to give Jessie her lesson today.

When the song ended Jessie began clapping and jumping up and down. "I want to play like that! Will I be able to play like that one day?" she asked.

"You will. I bet you'll be even better."

"Yay!" She smiled at him and then ran over to Wes, who hugged her. From there she went to Braden, who held her. He looked over Jessie's head at Wes, and damned if he didn't feel the love from the three of them all the way across the room.

Wes stood and ruffled Jessie's hair. "Come on, kiddo. I promised your aunt I would have you over there before dinner."

The little girl gave Braden a kiss goodbye before shouting, "Bye, Gavin! Thank you!"

Wes thanked him as well and then the two of them left. The door hardly clicked closed before Braden asked, "What's wrong with you?"

Damn it. He could never get one past Braden. "I've been asking myself the same thing about you since the moment we met." Gavin turned sideways and ran his fingers down the keys.

"Funny, man. How are things with your family?" Braden asked.

"Why do you insist on talking about them every time I'm with you?

Are you going to start charging me for your services, and if so, aren't I supposed to have a couch to lie on?"

"Maybe," Braden replied, simply. Obviously he wasn't going to take Gavin's bait and change the subject.

"It is what it is. Why hash it out?" Gavin shrugged. Talking about it wouldn't change things. His father was still losing his mind and his mom still thought he was going to Hell.

"Fine, then we'll talk about your love life. You need to get laid."

Gavin stopped playing. He hated how Braden assumed that Gavin hadn't. That he'd stayed home the day Braden came over and noticed the bite mark. "How do you know I haven't?"

"Because I know you."

Ouch. Gavin stood. "Listen, I better head out." He loved his friend, but he wanted this conversation over. "And mind your own business. Settling down has made you a gossip."

Shaking his head, Braden stood, too. "You mean a nosy bastard, but I've always been that. You're my friend. I care about you."

And he maybe felt a little bit of guilt that things hadn't worked out between them. That's the way Braden was, though. Gavin hated it now as much as he had then. Somehow he'd always made Braden feel like he needed to take care of Gavin.

"I know. But I'm a grown man. I can figure out what I need for my life."

Braden nodded and clapped him on the shoulder. "Then do it."

Chapter Fourteen

"Excuse me." Gavin went to the left, and Mason the right. Considering they were walking in opposite directions, it meant Gavin's left was Mason's right. So Mason went the other way, just as Gavin did the same.

"You stay," Mason teased Gavin as he worked his way around him behind the bar. It was Friday night and they'd been like this the whole time—awkward, which in itself was awkward as hell. Mason hadn't been that way around another man since he was a fumbling teenager.

The bar stayed steady the whole night. He and Gavin stayed fairly quiet, almost tiptoeing around each other although Mason didn't really know why.

By the time the bar closed he was about done with it. Mason locked up while Gavin wiped down the tables. The thing was, Mason had always been stubborn. With Gavin being standoffish, it made him the same. So instead of saying anything, he started to count down the register. When he looked up the next time, Gavin came out from the back, probably from the bathroom.

"I'm done here. I just need to grab something from my office and we can head out." Mason made sure to lock down his office like he did every night before making a quick stop to wash the day's work from his hands.

When he stepped into the hallway he heard the soft sound of the guitar. Slowly, Mason made his way toward the sound in the main area of the bar. Gavin sat in a chair on the stage, with his head down, playing.

Mason couldn't see his face but he could tell by Gavin's body language how much he and the music were connecting. It made him smile, though he wasn't really sure why. Maybe because he wasn't sure Gavin had ever connected with another human being the way he did with music.

Without a word, Mason made his way over. He sat the same way he had the first time Gavin played, with the chair backward and his eyes on the man. His hair fell in his face as his fingers danced along the cords as though they had a mind of their own. As though the guitar and Gavin's hand worked together.

It was a beautiful sight.

Mason no sooner thought the words before Gavin glanced up. He startled slightly, obviously not having realized he had an audience. "Shit. Sorry."

"Don't stop," Mason told him. Gavin's brows pulled together but he still did as Mason said—he continued to play the soft, acoustic melody. "What's wrong with you today? Hell, what was wrong with you the other day, too?"

For a second he thought Gavin would stop playing. His fingers fumbled but he quickly found his rhythm again. "Your ex, what's the deal with him?"

So that's what this was about? Jealousy? It only rang partially true. "Why do you want to know?"

"Because I fucked you the night before. I know exactly what it was—a fuck—but I also don't want to play games. I don't want to get in the middle if you two could work things out." His fingers fumbled again. And maybe what he said was part of the truth, but Mason could see Gavin was jealous. Damned if he didn't almost like that.

"We won't. My family and Isaac are close. I've known him my whole life. We dated for a few years. We're friends and we get along. We both wanted the same things so it worked. Months before I did, Isaac found out I'm adopted. I don't know how and don't give a shit. All I know was he didn't tell me. There's no chance we're getting back together."

Gavin's playing quieted.

"Don't stop," Mason said again. Gavin's forehead wrinkled but he picked up the music again.

"Can you blame him? It wasn't really his place."

Mason crossed his arms over the back of the chair. "You trying to talk me into getting back together with my ex or what?"

"No, he's an asshole. You know that's the truth, though."

And Mason did. It wasn't Isaac's responsibility to tell him. That belonged to his parents. "Maybe it was the excuse I needed to move on. Just like telling my family I won't be moving back to Denver to take care of the restaurants—I used the truth about my adoption as a way to tell them I wasn't going back. Isaac and I...hell the sex was always good, but—"

Gavin hit a wrong note. Yep, he was jealous. Mason grinned.

"But... This makes me sound like a bastard, but Isaac was always the life I tried to force myself to have. We both have business degrees and we both worked for my family. He was another thing that just happened. It was easy so we kept it going. That's all it ever was."

"Does he know that?" Gavin asked.

"He's in denial." Mason winked at him. "Let's keep this little game of tit for tat going. Why don't you tell me why you were late on Wednesday? Why have you been in a shitty mood since then?"

***

"Tit for tat, huh?" Gavin stalled. Talking about his family made him feel weak. It pissed him off and made guilt eat him alive at the same time. He didn't want to go through any of those emotions with Mason, especially not all three of them.

"Yeah. For some reason you turn me into a chatty motherfucker."

He wanted to chat? Gavin could chat. "I gave Jessie a piano lesson today. It made me realize how much I miss playing. I used to play at a few dueling piano bars."

Mason didn't reply. He didn't look away from Gavin, either. *Not gonna work, asshole,* his eyes said every time Gavin caught them.

"You have a way of getting what you want, don't you?"

"Hopefully, I do with you. That's all I'm worried about right now."

Gavin continued to play. Looking down he watched his fingers, thankful he had this thing that he loved so damn much. Music had saved him many times in his life. "My father…he asked about family. If I had a wife and had given him grandchildren, because he and Mom always wanted them. I opened my mouth to remind him but she cut me off. Made up a story about women who would be lucky to have me. We talked about the teaching job she pretended I still have and they said how proud they are of me and I…let it go. I just fucking let it go."

Gavin fought to tune out his own words, to concentrate on the music because it was the one love he always had. "I just fucking decided I was done quietly living my life. Done feeling guilty about who I am. That's what I came here for—a fresh start; and all I did was keep my mouth shut. Afterward she told me this was a silver lining in Dad's illness. His mind is going so that makes it easier to pretend. So he won't have to die knowing that he'll never see me again."

Because while his father would be in Heaven—Gavin would be in Hell.

Gavin shook his head. "Stop making me do this. I managed to escape my talk with Braden today, yet I come here and you manage to pry it all out of me." He didn't want to work through the fact that he'd been willing to share something with Mason that he hadn't with his oldest friend.

When Mason didn't reply, Gavin looked over at him—watched him stretch out his long legs and stand. Watched him move the chair to the side and walk over to him. Watched as Mason stopped in front of Gavin. As he touched one hand, then the other, stopping Gavin from playing.

"Now, he wants me to stop." Gavin tried to lighten the moment but

Mason ignored it.

He took the guitar from Gavin's hand and set it on the ground, and then said, "I like you, Teach."

He liked Mason as well. "You don't know me."

"So? I know you're sexy. I know you're a teacher and your parents have a fucked up idea of what the world is about. I know you love music and that you like to help people, which is an admirable quality. You're fun to be around, and you tell me things when I try to force them out of you. It's like you trust me, and that means something to me. I also know you're thirty years old and you're trying to figure out what the hell you really want out of your life, just like I am." Mason shrugged. "You're a good fuck, too. I know that."

Gavin laughed. He liked that Mason tried to level the heavy with a joke. His mind went back to what Braden said earlier—when Gavin told him he could figure out what he wanted for his life, Braden told him to do that. He'd been right. "Yeah, I guess I am." And then, "I like you, too, boss." He did. With Mason he felt a little less lost—or maybe just that he wasn't lost alone.

"Then I guess there's only one thing for us to do." Mason nodded for Gavin to stand and he did.

"And what's that?"

"Well, since we're both on this kick to experience life, and to figure out what we want...and since we both want each other, I figure that means we don't have much choice than to go on this ride together. Might crash and burn or might go for a joyride and then decide it's not our thing, but I'm sure we'll have a whole hell of a lot of fun in the process."

Gavin got exactly what Mason was saying. They weren't making any promises. Who knew what would happen? They hardly knew each other, but they liked what they knew so far. They had good chemistry and had a good time together. Maybe it would be something, but maybe it wouldn't. But he agreed they'd have fun testing the waters.

"Well…since we don't have a choice and all."

Mason cocked that brow of his at Gavin and smiled. Damned if Gavin didn't feel good. Better than he remembered feeling in a long time.

Chapter Fifteen

Mason followed Gavin to his house. Not that the couch in his office wasn't fun and all, but this time he wanted to fuck in a bed. Or against the wall, over the counter, or anything else they could think of. He just wanted it somewhere other than his bar.

He got his chance, because the second they walked into Gavin's house, the man was all over him. The kiss was sloppy and urgent but he didn't care. It was full of one hundred percent hunger, and that's all he gave a shit about.

They stumbled over a rug and almost fell. Mason laughed into Gavin's neck as he bit him there.

"You and those teeth."

"I like to bite." He nipped Gavin's skin again and Gavin groaned before pushing Mason against the closed front door. He hit hard, the knob jamming him in the side, but that was another thing he didn't care about.

"This fucking jaw of yours. So damn hot." Mason ran his tongue down Gavin's jawline.

And then Gavin dropped down in front of him, and Mason didn't care about much of anything except for the man's mouth.

"I didn't get to taste you last time." Gavin pushed his shirt up and kissed Mason's stomach. Mason ripped it off for him as Gavin continued to lick, kiss and suck at this skin.

"Then do it now." Mason ran a hand through Gavin's hair, and then watched it flop back down.

Gavin ripped the button through the hole before unzipping Mason's pants. He was already painfully hard, and eager to have Gavin's mouth on him. Mason leaned forward, his crotch right in front of Gavin's face. Since his jeans were only unbuttoned and unzipped there wasn't great access, but he held Gavin's head as the man sucked him through his boxer-briefs. "I like you down there. Now, take my clothes off."

Gavin shoved at Mason's pants and underwear, pushed them down until his prick sprung free—his clothes not going any farther than right under his ass and balls. "That's good enough for now," he told Gavin and then cursed when Gavin went right in for the deep throat.

"Holy fuck. Who'd have thought? I should have had you do this the first night."

"Sucking dick is a whole lot quicker. I got a lot more practice with it." And then he took Mason deep again. All the way back. Mason's balls touched Gavin's chin before he pulled off and then licked and sucked the head.

His whole body vibrated from the inside out as he listened to the sucking sound of Gavin going down on him. He loved a man on his knees. Loved being on them, too. There was something so powerful in sex. So demanding and owning that made Mason feel like he could conquer the world.

Like Isaac, he liked to win, too, but in bed—fucking—if he did everything right, both parties won. "Jack me off and suck on my balls. Show me what you can do."

Gavin did just that. Mason squeezed his eyes shut, fighting off the urge to orgasm. He almost never had one without penetration unless it was just his own hand, and even then there was also something inside him, too—fingers, a toy; they both worked for Mason.

But right now he didn't need that. He had a man on his knees who would suck him off and then fuck him, so he enjoyed the feel of the hot mouth on his balls. As his balls filled Gavin's mouth, he felt breath on his cock, and damned if it didn't make that urge to come hit him again.

He opened his eyes, looking down at Gavin. "I know I'm always telling you to kiss me, but right now, now's when I need you to fuck me."

He pulled Gavin to his feet. "Maybe one kiss first." Mason took his mouth. He felt Gavin unbuttoning his jeans as their tongues battled.

Gavin pushed his pants down about as far as Mason's before he grabbed their shafts, squeezing them together and thrusting forward. "Fuck." Mason thrust, too. Their tongues fucked each other's mouths as their dicks rubbed against each other.

"Over the couch." Mason pushed Gavin away. Grabbed his wallet and tossed it at the man, who caught it. He pulled his pants down farther but didn't take the time to step out of them. Right now he just wanted to be full.

He heard a package rip and figured Gavin found the condom and small packet of lube in his wallet. There was a thump, and Mason looked down to see his wallet hit the floor.

The condom rapper fell next, and then he felt a cold, wet finger at his asshole. When it pushed inside, the muscles in his whole body released tension. He relaxed, that need inside him so ready to be sated.

There was one finger, then another. "Come on, teach. I'm waiting." Mason pushed back into him and then the fingers were gone, replaced by the thick head of Gavin's prick.

As he worked himself inside, Mason's eyes rolled back, his ass pushed closer. This was exactly what he wanted.

***

"Hold up...." Gavin kept completely still. If he didn't he would embarrass himself. Mason's ass squeezed him in just the right way, a tight, hot fist engulfing his erection.

When he felt like he had at least ten percent control over his body, Gavin pulled out and then thrust forward again. Mason met each of his movements with one of his own.

"I fucking love that—the feel of thighs slapping against the back of mine—of body slamming into me from behind."

Damned if Gavin didn't, too. He'd always enjoyed sex. He'd had some pretty good sex in his lifetime, even if there hadn't been a lot of it. But still, this was different... This was power. It was possession.

He wrapped his arm around Mason's body and reached for his cock. Mason's hand was there already. "I want to do it," he said before leaning forward and biting into the back of Mason's neck, the way the man did with him. He'd never done that before, used his teeth on someone like that, but it made the lust overtake him. Made him tip closer to the edge that he couldn't wait to jump from.

"Make me do it."

Gavin realized he liked that—liked the thought of being the one to control Mason jerking himself off, so he wrapped his hand over the other man's. The movements weren't as smooth as they could be since they hadn't used any lube, but he didn't have it in him to stop. Gavin guided Mason's hand, worked it up and down his own rod as he thrust. Hard. Then harder. Fast. Then faster.

"Jesus Christ," Mason ground out. Gavin almost stopped moving at that, years of growing up in a religious home making him automatically respond to the name, but then he felt Mason jerk. Felt the thick come slide between their fingers as Mason fucked their hands.

Mason's ass clinched around him, causing Gavin to shoot, too. He thrust his way through it as they both still worked Mason's cock. And then he dropped against Mason, Gavin's chest rising and falling against Mason's back as they both breathed heavily.

They were silent as they caught their breath. Gavin was still half-hard as he held onto the condom to pull out.

"Natural born top and you didn't even know it." Mason turned around, forcing Gavin to stand up straight.

He didn't know about that, but he did know he sure as hell enjoyed fucking Mason. "If you say so." He stepped away. "I think we might need to try it a few more times to make sure."

Mason laughed. Gavin pulled his pants up but didn't button them. "I need to get rid of this."

He went to the bathroom and tossed the condom. When he came back into the living room, Mason was stretching.

"You can crash here if you want." His own words somehow struck him. He'd never spent the whole night with a man other than Braden. And hell, maybe he shouldn't even have asked Mason. They were only fucking, and spending the night sounded close to relationship territory, but he didn't take the statement back. He didn't want to.

"Thank Christ. You took it out of me. If you would have made me drive home, I probably would have fallen asleep at the wheel and it would have been all your fault."

"Made, huh? I thought you were the boss?"

Mason had already pulled up his pants as well, but Gavin noticed semen on his stomach. He liked it there.

"You're right. You couldn't make me leave if you tried. Now lead the way to your bedroom. There's always a small window with me between orgasm and passing out."

Chapter Sixteen

Mason fell into an easy pattern with Gavin over the next two weeks. Gavin kept up his lessons with Jessie. On his days off he still sometimes ended up at the bar, even if just for a little while, to visit. They worked together, and a few nights a week Mason ended up at Gavin's for the night so the man could fuck his brains out.

Mason had no reason to complain about how they spent their time together.

Being around Gavin was easy, comfortable, and Mason liked easy and comfortable.

On a slow, Saturday night Mason approached Gavin as he stood behind the bar, filling a mug of dark brew. "Wanna sneak into my office for a blow job?" He whispered as he passed.

The mug slipped out of Gavin's hand, shattering on the floor. Beer went everywhere as Mason let out a loud laugh. "I'm kidding, teach." Or was he? He wouldn't mind a quickie with Gavin on his knees.

When Gavin met his eyes, Mason saw fire there and realized he hadn't shocked Gavin. Mason turned him on. He leaned against the counter. Mason kept his voice low when he spoke. "There's a closet freak in there. I like a little kink."

"Kink? Who doesn't like a little kink?" Mason laughed at the sound of Cooper's voice behind him.

"You're going to scandalize him." Braden spoke up next as he and Wes sat down. Noah and Cooper took stools beside them.

"That's the plan." Mason grabbed the broom from the corner. "Excuse me while I clean up the mess Gavin made while being properly scandalized."

His lover shook his head but Mason saw a smile tease his lips. "We have customers."

"No one's paying attention to us except these guys. Well, them and Rich down the bar. He wants his beer."

Gavin seemed to take Mason's hint. He grabbed another mug and filled it before walking it down the bar to the waiting customer.

"Out causing trouble?" Mason asked as he first cleaned up the broken glass.

"Braden's always looking for it." Wes rested his arms on the bar.

"Funny, Coop is, too," Noah added.

It was Cooper who got a smirk on his face that told Mason he had a comeback. "It's not our fault if we're more fun than the two of you."

The four of them laughed. They were a good group of men. Mason liked them a lot. He had since first moving to Blackcreek.

It was already close to eleven when the foursome came in. Gavin gave them a pitcher of beer and he and Mason chatted with them off and on as they helped the customers who trickled in and out of the bar.

A little more than an hour later, only a few people lingered in the bar. A man and woman sitting at a table in the back corner and two guys playing pool. Mason checked on them to see if anyone needed a refill, and when they didn't he joined Gavin, who spoke to their friends.

"Looking a little slow in here," Braden teased Mason. "I thought Gavin was here because you needed extra help."

"Jesus, Braden. You and that damn mouth of yours," Wes replied.

"You like my mouth."

Mason had no doubt that Wes did. He also didn't mind Braden trying to bust his balls. "It was a little bit of both. We're usually busy, but looks like you chased everyone out tonight. And Gavin...hell, he's nice to look at. That's the perk of having him around." He winked at his lover.

"I get that a lot." Gavin shrugged, playing along.

Mason stood beside Gavin at the bar. The sleeves of his shirt pulled up when he crossed his arms, stretching over his muscles. He didn't like the attention on him. He played it off well, but Mason could tell.

"What happened to the live music?" Noah asked as he finished the beer in the bottom of his glass. "Didn't you used to have it on the weekends?"

"Yeah, but it was a lot of work, finding bands and booking them. It's the music man's job now. He'll no doubt be better at it than I was." He nudged Gavin. "Hey, I like that. Now I don't know if I want to call you teach or the music man. I'm hoping eventually I can get Gavin to play here."

Gavin's attention turned to Mason. He had a strange look in his eye, almost like what Mason said he hadn't expected. He wasn't sure why. He'd told Gavin from the beginning he could help with the music.

"Yeah?" Gavin asked.

"Of course. You sure as shit sound better than most of the people I had coming in and out of here. I'm still expecting those lessons."

The longer Gavin looked at him, Mason realized what it meant. It was gratitude. Mason could appreciate that quality. Most of the people he knew went about life with a cocky attitude, like their shit didn't stink. Not Gavin. He wasn't sure what he did to deserve it, but damned if it didn't make him reach over, wrap his arm around Gavin and pull him close. He pressed a kiss to his forehead before setting him free again.

***

When Gavin had been a kid, he wasn't uncomfortable with public displays of affection. It was an argument he and Braden often had. When they were in high school, as much as he'd been honored Braden asked him to the dance, he'd been uncomfortable the whole time.

He tried not to show it. Hated that it was true. At the time he thought maybe being with Braden would show him it was okay to be who he was.

Even after they graduated and moved away, he found himself automatically flinching away when Braden would try to touch him in public. It wasn't something that made Gavin proud, but it was true.

There hadn't been a bone in his body that made him want to pull away from Mason just now.

Sure, that had to do with being older now, and probably because of everything he'd lost along the way. Why the hell should he deny himself the chance at a normal relationship on top of it? But part of him wondered if he just didn't like Mason's hands on him as well.

"I'll see what I can figure out," Gavin finally responded to what Mason had said. When the man first brought it up, he hadn't taken it seriously. Especially since it hadn't been mentioned since.

It was a responsibility Gavin wanted, though. He would love to bring live music to the bar, as long as it was the right kind of music.

"Are you going to play, too?" Wes asked.

"I didn't know you played," Cooper added.

"Yep. He can pick any instrument up and play it," Braden said. "He's giving Jess piano lessons."

From there that led the conversation to Braden and Wes's little girl and how their family was doing, which was fine by Gavin. He wasn't sure how he felt about playing at the bar—in front of Mason and everyone they knew. He hadn't done anything like that for years.

"You didn't answer," Mason whispered in his ear. Damn the man.

"They changed the subject."

"And you're looking for excuses. Seize the day, remember? If you're trying to figure out what you want in life, you need to grab the bull by the fucking horns and do so." He popped Gavin with a towel and then walked away.

Gavin stood there, watching him go. It seemed Mason Alexander had a habit of saying exactly what Gavin needed to hear.

Chapter Seventeen

Mason hit ignore on his cell. It made him a jackass. The knowledge hadn't escaped him, but he wasn't in the mood to go home right now.

He knew that's what his mother wanted—for him to come home. To pretend like nothing had changed. Maybe she even hoped that they could go back to the way things were—him working for them, being with Isaac, and never knowing that he had a mom out there who had given him away and didn't even know who his father was.

It probably shouldn't be—not at his age—but it was a tough pill to swallow.

"Where are you taking me today?" Naked, he walked back over to Gavin's bed and fell into it. Once they'd closed the bar last night, he hadn't been able to think of a reason not to go home with Gavin, so he had.

Not that he'd tried to think of a reason.

"I didn't know I was taking you anywhere." Gavin buried his head in the pillow.

"I can't believe you're not a morning person. You're a teacher. Doesn't that mean you're used to getting up early and pushing lazy kids into being productive at an early hour?"

At that, Gavin peeked over the arm that covered his face and said, "It's a lie. Teachers fake it. I don't have to fake it anymore."

His words were a joke, but Mason heard the sadness in them. "You're up, Teach. I took you to jump out of a fucking plane. Where are you taking me? I thought we were supposed to be experiencing life. And you have a lot to live up to, just so you know. I'm not sure anything can top skydiving."

"Music," Gavin groaned.

"What's that, Mumbles? I didn't hear you." Mason swatted his ass and then stood.

At that, Gavin sat up. "I said music. And did you forget we didn't go to bed until after three this morning?"

"Then get me off sooner next time, if you want to go to bed. Now you've hooked me with the music talk. Where are we going?"

A slow smile spread across Gavin's face, and then he pushed out of bed. Apparently he hooked more than just Mason.

"It's possibly the band geek in me talking, because it's definitely *not* skydiving, but there's this show...the Boulder Music Festival. It's this weekend—music all day, all weekend. I've always wanted to go." Gavin paused a second before nodding. "Get dressed, boss. That's where I'm taking you today."

Mason didn't look at Gavin and see a man who lacked confidence.

It wasn't that, but he never held himself quite as tall, never spoke with as much authority as he did when he spoke about music.

Mason envied him for that—that he had one thing that he loved so much. Mason enjoyed his bar. He enjoyed working for something, but he'd never loved anything the way Gavin so clearly loved music.

He enjoyed sharing that with him, wanted to see Gavin in his element.

Mason showered while Gavin packed up a few things for their day. Then Gavin got ready, and less than forty-five minutes later they were on their way to Boulder.

The ride was different than the first one they'd taken, the conversation comfortable the way it was when you really start to know someone. They fought over what to listen to in the car, and Gavin told Mason he had shit taste, when really Mason couldn't care less what they listened to. He just liked to get Gavin riled up.

Music already filled the air when they got to the concert.

"I got it," Gavin told him when they made it to the entrance. He took out his wallet and bought two tickets.

Mason waited until the tickets were purchased before he spoke. "I didn't pay for you when we went skydiving."

"So?"

"See, now I feel like an asshole." Mason nudged him with his arm as they walked inside.

"Don't. I did it because I want to. Plus, that was before."

Mason quirked a brow at him. "Before what?" He knew exactly

what Gavin meant.

"Before I was fucking you."

Mason glanced over at Gavin and nudged him again. He crossed his arms but wouldn't look at Mason. It didn't surprise him, really. It was a nice gesture, but wasn't really needed. "Just because we're fucking doesn't mean you have to buy my concert ticket."

"Is it a problem that I wanted to?" This time Gavin did look his way.

It had been different with Isaac. Despite the fact that they'd been together for so long, they didn't really do things like that. Sure, if the family went out to dinner he or Isaac might pay, but Mason could tell it was different for Gavin. It was new and somehow felt like more.

He thought for a minute as they made their way through the sea of people. The closer they got the louder they had to speak. "Nah, not a problem. I think I might like that you want to date me. Next time, it's my treat."

Gavin pushed a hand through his hair and gave Mason a small nod. "Yeah, okay. I can handle that."

Funny, after all the shit that went down with him recently, the last thing Mason figured he would do was get involved with someone. It had been a little over three months since he and Isaac had permanently broken up. They'd cooled off when Mason moved to Blackcreek, which had made his lie about a break-up making him buy his bar easier. But since he told him they were over for good, just a quarter of a year.

This was easy, though. For some reason spending time with Gavin was easy. Mason could use a little of that.

"We should do this every week. Something fun...different."

"Yeah," Gavin replied. "I'd like that."

***

"Listen to that." Gavin grabbed Mason's arm and pulled him close. He lowered his mouth to Mason's ear as he spoke. "Do you hear that? Listen to the way the guitar and the piano sound together. It's almost like they're sparring, yet working together at the same time. Do you hear how one will ease off when the other goes for it, and vice versa?"

Gavin loved that, loved everything about music and how it made him feel alive. For most of his life, it had been the only thing to make him feel that way.

"I hear it," Mason replied, close to his ear. But he didn't hear it the same way Gavin did. If he had, there would have been more life in his voice.

"Close your eyes," Gavin told him.

"What?"

"Close your fucking eyes. Come on, before it's over."

Mason frowned but did as he was told. Gavin ran completely off of instinct here, not sure why he needed so badly for Mason to hear what he did. He slid behind him, wrapping his arms around Mason. "Try and tune out everyone else and just listen."

"Gav—"

"Shh. Listen." Gavin drummed his thumbs on Mason's chest, trying to match the beat of the music, tapping harder when the music went louder, and letting off when it went softer.

Before he realized it, his eyes were closed, too. He kept ahold of Mason from behind, and listened along with him. "Piano," he whispered close to Mason's ear. Gavin let the music filter through him, hoped he could make it filter through Mason as well. "Guitar," he added when the guitar took the lead. He loved bands that played with a piano. It added such an incredible dimension to the music.

His thumb still played the tune on Mason's chest. Gavin concentrated on the beat, tried to follow it, tried to make it sink into Mason. "Both of them here. This is the battle, where they both are going for it."

Mason's hard body leaned backward into him. They molded together, people all around them, touching them, but they were somehow alone, too.

"Hear it?" He asked.

He felt Mason's words more than he heard them, felt the vibration through his hands that lay on Mason's chest. "Yeah, I hear it."

And then the song was over. Gavin dropped his arms but didn't move away. Mason turned his head, tilted it up. Gavin dropped his head so his ear would be closer to Mason's mouth. "Christ, that was sexy. I don't think I've ever really heard music like that before."

"That's because you've never really listened to it before. You're never alone if you have music."

Hell, that sounded much more needy than he meant it to sound. "It's not—"

"Let's go, music man." Mason grabbed his hand and pulled Gavin through the crowd. They kept going until they were on the outskirts of the open field. They could still hear the music but could actually speak without yelling, and there wasn't a throng of people against them.

"Sit down," Mason told him, and Gavin found himself doing what he said. He went down on the ground and then Mason sat between his legs. "Do that again. Make me feel the music."

So he did. Gavin wrapped his arms around Mason. He kept his mouth close to the man's ear, humming or whispering the beat of the songs. He tapped on Mason's chest, playing the music on him. It was erotic as hell. It was something more than that, too.

He really liked this man, and he wasn't quite sure how he felt about that.

Chapter Eighteen

Mason had been putting off going to lunch with his family. When he first made what they all considered his temporary move to Blackcreek, he'd gone weekly. Whether it should or not, that all changed when he found out the truth of his adoption. Being busy with work was true, but it was also a good excuse.

It was strange to suddenly feel out of place in the environment that had always been his home. With the people who were his family. Yes, there were parts of him that never totally felt like he fit. Not unwelcome, or as though he didn't belong—just different. But in other ways, home was the place he always felt welcome as well.

He was still welcome there. They wanted him there. The hang-up belonged strictly with Mason. He got that, but there was something holding him back. Something that made it near impossible for him to get over the fact that they'd looked him in the eyes and lied to him his entire life.

Considering it was Monday, his day off, and Gavin planned to make the trip home to see his family, Mason figured now was as good a time as any.

They'd talked about it in the car on the way home from the concert last night, and so he hadn't stayed at Gavin's, either. The second he'd gone home to his empty place, he'd second-guessed that decision. Why the hell would he want to stay home alone when he could spend the night with Gavin's body wrapped around his?

But it's exactly what they'd done, and now he pulled into the driveway of his parent's oversized house with a knot in his gut.

For a minute, he sat in his SUV looking at the home he'd been raised in. He'd lived here as long as he could remember—since he was a child. Every memory he had in this home had been a happy one. They played games here and had dinner together every night.

He'd come out to his parents in this home, and they'd hugged him and said he'd always be their son, that they would always love him no matter what.

Did it make him a prick that he couldn't help but wonder why they also didn't love him enough to tell him the truth?

Before he spent the whole day out here feeling sorry for himself, Mason got out of the SUV and headed for the house. It had six bedrooms and three-and-a-half baths, when the most people who had ever lived it in at a time was Mason and his parents.

Before Mason had the chance to go in, his father opened the door. "Hey, son. Glad to see you could make it." He reached out his hand and they shook. Shook fucking hands. It had been like that since he found out, when his dad had always been a hugger before.

"Hey, Dad. How's everything going?"

"Good, good. The doctor has me exercising every day. I have to run on that damned treadmill for at least thirty minutes a night."

"That *damned* treadmill is good for him." Mason's mom came into the foyer. Unlike his dad, she pulled him into a hug.

"It's good to see you," she told him.

"It's good to see you, too." And it was. Maybe that's what made it so hard.

Lunch was already on the table when he got there. Mason walked with his parents into the second dining room. They used the first for when they had company. It was more for show, while the second was more intimate.

The table only sat six. It was marble, with fresh flowers in the middle. They were replaced every few days. It had been like that as long as Mason could remember.

"I made salmon. I hope that's okay." His father pulled out the chair for his mom as she spoke.

And just saying "salmon" was an understatement. They had fish, rice, and asparagus, her butter cream sauce on the side. They also had raspberry walnut salad, as well as a bottle of wine.

For lunch. Mason liked to keep healthy, and he always paid attention to what he put in his body, but he couldn't comprehend going through this much trouble for lunch. "You didn't have to do all of this, Mom." She must have spent half the morning preparing their food.

"Doing all of what?"

"Never mind." He kissed her cheek and sat down.

They dug into their meal, mostly in silence. Mason couldn't stop his eyes from studying them both. He used to think he looked like his dad, but now he knew that couldn't be true.

It was a shock to his system—to always know where he came from only to find out he never really had. Only to find out that he had someone's genes inside him, had a family he didn't know.

What would they think of Mason? Would they enjoy sitting down in his bar for a beer, or would they not be able to accept who he was? Did he look like his mom or his dad? Have siblings who wondered about him?

He'd wanted that so bad as a kid, wanted brothers and sisters, and now he possibly had them.

"What do you have going on the rest of the day?" his mom asked about halfway through their meal.

"Nothing, really. Why?"

"It's just…we miss having you around. Your father has to run an errand for the restaurant, and we thought you guys could spend some time together. You can help him take care of some business and then come back here, for dinner."

It was then he realized they cornered him. Maybe that wasn't the right word, but they had a very specific plan for today, only they hadn't let Mason in on it until now. "Mom, I—"

"Please, Mason. I just…" She wiped her eyes and guilt immediately swam through him. Damn it. No matter what, he didn't want to hurt them. What harm could one day make?

"Yeah, sure. That sounds like a nice day." He felt like an asshole, because it didn't at all.

***

"I have a surprise for you." Gavin's mom beamed at him from where she sat in her chair, knitting."

"Oh yeah? What is it?" He set her mug of hot tea on the table beside her. Gavin had no idea how she could drink hot tea in the summer, but she always did. Sunshine, rain, snow, heat wave, it didn't matter to her. She liked to drink her hot tea, and that's just the way it was.

It's one of the things he remembered so fondly from his childhood. Hot tea was her cure for everything. Any time Gavin was sick she made him drink tea, with honey and lemon.

"I spoke with Dennis from church. I explained to him that you'd left your job and have been looking for another one."

Ice injected into his veins. Gavin hadn't lost his job; he'd had no choice in leaving (though he could have fought it). And he wasn't looking for a job. Not here, and not at her church. "I have a job, Mom. It probably won't be what I do forever, but it works for now. I'm happy at Creekside."

He sat in the chair across from her even though he knew this couldn't possibly go well.

She set her knitting on her lap. "Gavin...you're promoting sin. Pushing alcohol...it's not...it's not how we raised you."

They hadn't raised him to be gay, either, but he was.

"I know things are difficult right now, but I believe they'll get better. You just need help getting on the right track. Move home. Come work at the church. You can start attending again with me, and see how things go. I—"

"That would never work. It's important that I come home and help you more. I'm sure it's a struggle, but I can't move back. I can't go to work at the church. I'm happy where I am. You should come see the house sometime. It's a great little place, and Braden's letting me rent it for cheap. There are a few things that need a little work, but Mason and I are going to start fixing it up a little so—"

"Who is that? Mason?" She already had knowledge in her voice. She had to know she wouldn't want the answer.

"He owns the bar I work at. He's a good friend."

Shaking her head, she tried to stand but then went back into the chair again.

"Here, let me help you," Gavin told her but she waved him off, tried again and made it up.

"I don't understand you. I don't. Think about what you're risking. We only want what's best for you. Is that too much to ask? We want what's best for you and what's best for the family.

She didn't want Gavin to be who he was. "Mom—"

"No. I can't do this right now, Gavin. Not with everything going on with your father. If you can't…if you aren't willing to do what's best for yourself and this family, I'm going to have to ask you to leave."

When she turned away from him, Gavin had no choice except to get up and leave. He wasn't sure what made him dial his phone before driving, but he did. Maybe Mason would need him to work at the bar.

"Hello." There was laughter in the background, the unmistakable voice of Isaac.

"Hey."

More noise in the background. "I'll be right back," Mason said to the people who were with him. Gavin could tell he went to another room before he said, "Sorry about that."

Anger ripped through him. He didn't have a right to be angry but he was. "It's okay. I'll let you go. I just wanted to say hi."

"No, it's okay. How are things with your family? Do you guys have plans for tonight?"

Gavin had told Mason earlier that he might stay the night with his mom. He'd figured they could use the time together, but he guessed not. Not since she'd told him to leave.

"Mase, I want to show you something when you're done." Isaac.

Gavin's anger skyrocketed. He probably wasn't even mad at Isaac, but he felt like it.

"I'll let you go," Gavin said.

"No, it's okay."

"Don't worry about it. I'll talk to you tomorrow. Have a good night." And then, like a child, he hung up the phone.

Chapter Nineteen

Mason fought an internal war all day.

He laughed in all the right places and smiled in the right ones. He followed his father along as they took care of some business for the restaurants.

When employees approached him and told Mason they missed him, he returned the sentiment, because it was true. He missed the people. Missed customers that he'd seen weekly since he was a child, or chefs who spent their career working for his father. Even though they owned more than one restaurant, and even though they'd always been insanely busy, his father treated his employees like family. Mason had tried to do the same.

And he knew from the start that's what this entire trip down memory lane was about.

They wanted him to see what he left behind. They wanted him to come back, even though they hadn't asked yet.

"Should we go have a glass of wine in the garden?" his mom asked, once they finished dinner.

Mason shook his head. "I should probably be heading back."

"Come on, Mase. Enjoy the evening with us," Isaac prodded with a wink. The bastard. He knew exactly what he was doing.

"It's always so relaxing out there. We've always enjoyed our time in the garden, together as a family." The hurt in her voice stung, ripped through him like the lash from a whip. Christ, he didn't want to hurt her—didn't want to hurt any of them—but the wounds were fresh.

"For a little while. No drink, though. I'm good."

The gardens out back were his mom's favorite place. As a child, Mason remembered sitting outside with her for hours while she tended to her plants. They often sat at the table as a family. The metal on it twisted and turned, making vines that mimicked the plants she loved so much.

"Mason and I checked in at Fourth St. and Highland today. Both of them look good. When's the last time you stopped in to speak with Jeremy in Boulder?" Mason's dad asked Isaac.

"Last month. I made a trip down there. We've spoken on the phone since. They had a bad month—low numbers; but things are picking up. We need to put some thought into a meeting with Bryce in Durango. I'm worried about how things are going down there."

"Why?" Mason asked, and then immediately regretted the question. Durango was always harder for them because it was so damn far away. He'd always thought his parents should sell, but since his mom was born there, and it was the first restaurant they started, it had sentimental value.

"Money isn't coming in like it should, yet hours are high. They're busy, but the cash is going somewhere. We might need to let him go," Isaac replied.

"How do we know it's him? We need to figure out what's going on first." Which meant a trip to a city six hours away for who knew how long. There weren't many options on who could do it—his dad, Isaac or Mason.

Only, he had the bar now. He couldn't make a trip like that. "Shit." Mason groaned, and rubbed his hand over his face. He couldn't leave his family out to dry, either.

"We'll figure it out," his dad said as Mom nodded.

"Yeah, that's enough work talk for tonight."

Mason felt like he had a hand wrapped around his throat for the rest of the evening. He didn't like the idea of his dad traveling for business. He wasn't sure what made him feel it, but things were off where his dad was concerned. That left him two restaurants here and one in Boulder if Isaac went to Durango, and Mason didn't like that, either. His dad looked more tired than he used to. He didn't move around as fast.

Finally, when his brain wouldn't stop running around, Mason had enough. He pushed to his feet, "I'm tired. I still have a long drive ahead of me."

"Why don't you stay here?" There was a slight, pleading tone to his mother's voice.

"Not tonight. I need to stop in and make sure things are okay at the bar, anyway." Which was true. Mason had a hard time leaving it in control of someone else.

"I'll walk you out." Isaac stood as well.

Not in the mood to argue, he let it go and said goodbye to his parents. They made it all the way to his SUV before Isaac asked, "Still letting the bartender fuck you?"

Christ, he should have known this was coming. "Do we really have to do this again? You're starting to look needy." That was something he knew Isaac wouldn't be able to handle.

"No, I just know what I want. There's nothing wrong with that."

Mason stifled a yawn. He didn't have time for this. "Have a good one, Isaac. I need to get home." He climbed into his SUV and turned it on. When Isaac knocked on the window, he groaned but then rolled it down.

"Don't stress on Durango. I'll figure it out."

He cocked his head a little and looked at his ex. He hadn't expected that one. "You know I'll still worry, but thanks."

He went to put the vehicle into gear when Isaac spoke again. "What is it? That you see in the bartender, I mean?"

Mason leaned back in the seat and let out a deep breath. "He's not really a bartender. He is, but he won't be forever. He teaches, and..." Mason shrugged. "He's a breath of fresh air. He could be jaded by the world but he isn't. He pays attention to things I never have. It's like he suddenly woke up and realized he's alive... It's incredible to experience." When he caught Isaac's eyes, the man looked at him like he'd never seen Mason before. It made his gut tense up. "And he fucks like a God. Best I've had in a long time."

He winked at Isaac, who shook his head. "Asshole. We know that's not true."

"Think what you will." He nodded at his ex and then drove away. He spent the whole drive worried about his parents and the business, and wondering why in the hell he was having such a hard time with this. In the back of his mind, Gavin was there, too, and he couldn't help but worry about how Gavin's day had gone, hoping it went better than his.

***

Gavin sat on his living room couch, in the dark.

She'd asked him to leave. He couldn't believe his mother had asked him to leave. No matter how many ups and downs they had over the years. No matter how many tears there were, or prayers that would never change who he was, and meetings with church members, and fears and anger over Braden when he was a kid, he'd never been asked to leave.

They loved him, they worried about him, but they would never cast him out.

In a way, she'd done that very thing tonight.

Gavin didn't move when he saw lights travel across the wall. Then heard a car door slam, and then finally a knock.

Damn it. There was no one it could be except Mason. If he was being honest, part of him was glad the man came here. His whole body went rigid when he thought about Mason spending time with Isaac, laughing with his family the way Gavin would never be able to do with a man he dated and his own parents.

And he really didn't like Isaac all that much.

But he also wasn't in the mood to see anyone tonight, either.

When the door opened behind him, he dropped his head against the back of the couch and mumbled, "Make yourself at home, why don't you?"

"What are you doing here? I thought you were staying with your family? And why in the hell are you sitting in the dark?" Mason closed the door, and then hit the light.

"If you didn't think I was home, then why did you come?"

"I stopped by the bar on my way home. Your house is between the bar and mine. I saw your car."

Gavin looked at the clock. "It's only nine. Wouldn't have figured you'd make it home so early."

Mason crossed his arms. "What in the hell is that supposed to mean?"

Damn it, he was being a prickly bastard, but he couldn't help it. The need to fight, to lash out, ripped through every inch of Gavin's body. This wasn't like him at all, but that didn't stop him from saying, "I don't know, you just sounded like you were having an awfully good time with Isaac. I'm surprised it's over so soon."

"Are you shitting me? What the hell is wrong with you?" Mason moved closer to him and Gavin pushed to his feet. He felt like he would overheat, like someone injected fire into his veins and it burned him from the inside out.

He stood right in front of Mason; by now, both men breathed heavily. "I know we haven't defined, whatever the hell this is we're doing, but I appreciate knowing if you're letting someone else fuck you at the same time that I am. He shows up at the bar and can't keep his eyes off you. And then he goes home with you that night. Oh, and he just so happens to be at your family's house with you, too. Fuck!" Gavin latched his hands together, behind his head, elbows facing forward. His eyes fell closed and he tried to calm down the storm trying to take him over.

What in the hell was wrong with him tonight?

"First of all, I told you there's not a chance that Isaac and I are getting back together. I don't lie. I can't handle people who do. I know he can be a prick, but he's my friend, and he's close to my family. He's at my parent's house—often. You're going to have to deal with that if we keep up *whatever the hell this is we're doing*," he threw Gavin's words back in his face. "If you can't trust me, then there's no reason for us to keep this up."

Guilt added to the hurricane blasting through his insides. Mason didn't deserve his wrath.

"Hey. What the hell is wrong? This isn't like you. If you have some shit you need to work through, I know of a better way to do it than this. Don't pick a fight with me because you're pissed at someone else. And what the hell, look at me." He grabbed Gavin's hands, prying them apart. When he did, Gavin opened his eyes, devastated from the category five that ravaged him.

"Fuck!" Gavin yelled again. He went to turn, but Mason grabbed his shirt in a tight fist and wouldn't let him go.

"Tell me."

"This isn't a game. You don't get to tell me what to do and then I just do it."

"Are you mad? You look like you're about ready to explode. You look like you want to hit me. Do you want to fight me?"

Gavin looked down to see his hands were in a fist. He shook them out, trying to figure out when he'd balled them that way. Trying to figure out what this was all about. He knew, but then…he'd always known how his parents felt, and he'd never reacted like this before, because Mason had been right. For a second there, he wanted to hit him—or someone. Anyone. He just wanted to let all the anger out that he kept trapped inside him.

"Nah, you won't hit me. You want to fuck me, that's what you want, isn't it? You want to fuck me hard, until you forget all the other stuff. Just screw it away and then go on about your life and pretend it doesn't exist. Pretend that you haven't been keeping it trapped inside you your whole damn life. I'm game, if you want."

Mason started to unbutton his pants.

"Stop," Gavin gritted out.

"Why? I like a hard fuck. We can pretend it's the same as you used to do. Fuck some random guy, except before it was your ass—get that anger out about who you are, get the need to fuck out of you so you're good for a while, and then we can go our separate ways."

His zipper went down, and then Mason started to pull at his own jeans.

"Stop," Gavin told him again, this time grabbing onto Mason's hands.

"What? You want to do it? Have at it. Take them off and then I'll turn my back to you so maybe it will feel like old times, because you won't have to look at me and remember you know me. Except for with

Braden. He's the only person you had that you actually cared about. Should I be jealous of him the way you are Isaac?"

Mason turned. Gavin's dick was painfully hard and he almost hated that fact. Hated that what Mason just said turned him on, because the truth in everything his lover just said was devastating.

"I'm waiting, music man. Or have you had enough living and you're done? Just going to go find a little school to teach at where you can forget you're gay? A few times a year when your dick won't stop aching you'll go let someone get you off before you keep on pretending you're someone else?"

Pain shattered Gavin's insides.

He wanted to fight.

Wanted to fuck.

Wanted to do everything Mason just said.

There was a sigh from Mason, and then calloused fingers holding Gavin's jaw so he couldn't look away. "Tell me what happened. You give me yours and I'll give you mine. That's what we're really doing here, right? Aren't we supposed to be living? Letting loose? Can't do that shit if you keep it all inside. Jump out of the plane, Gav."

It was those words that trapped him—or hell, maybe they set him free.

Gavin sat on the couch, and jumped.

Chapter Twenty

Mason had no fucking clue if he'd just done the right thing. All he knew was the Gavin he walked in on wasn't the Gavin he'd grown to know. Wasn't the man he sat listening to music with, or the one he'd gone on his hike with. He wasn't the man he'd let fuck him senseless.

He wanted that man back. And he wanted him to stay. He wanted to keep on forgetting his family and his responsibilities and keep having fun with Gavin while they figured out what they wanted.

Most of all, he wanted the pain gone from Gavin's eyes.

"I'm so fucking angry," Gavin finally said. "I've done everything right. When I was a kid, I tried to stop. I tried to force myself not to be gay. When I couldn't, when I met Braden, I did everything I could to make up for it. I went to church every week like they wanted me to. But it was never enough."

This time it was Mason's hands that fisted. What the fuck was wrong with his family that they would make him feel this way? *What the fuck is wrong with you? Your family accepts you and you can't get over the fact that they screwed up?*

"That's because it was a lie, Gav. A lie will never be enough because it's not real." He sat down next to the man, ran a hand through his wet hair. He'd showered before Mason got there. He could smell the soap and shampoo on him.

"Yeah…yeah, I realized that after a while."

"With Braden? Maybe I should be the one to be jealous."

Gavin shook his head. "We were never in love with each other. He just made it easy to pretend I was okay."

He wasn't going to let the subject veer. "You're not off the hook yet. Keep going."

"Bossy."

"And you like it." Mason sat back and waited.

"Things were already strained with Braden. We both knew we were just biding time. I went to see my family. They had a damned intervention waiting. They loved me. They believed in me. All that shit. I knew I was gay. Hell, I always had, but when I left from my visit, I focused on school more and more. Braden left and I was too busy to date. Then I graduated and was starting my career, and I was too busy to date again." Gavin ran a hand through his hair. "This talk would have been a whole hell of a lot easier if I had a guitar or something to play. Or maybe if you were distracting me."

"This is all stuff you've told me before. Why are you pissed right now?" Mason wasn't letting Gavin off that easily. He wanted to know everything about this man in a way he'd never experienced before.

Gavin didn't answer for over a minute. Mason could practically see

137

the frustration set in his body.

"Because I lived my life for them—hell, for everyone else, too. I did everything right and it wasn't enough. I lost my fucking job. My dad is losing his mind, and my own mother asked me to leave today. If I can't support my family and do the right thing by her and Dad by denying who I am, I'm not welcome in her home."

Mason knew that had to hurt. "No matter how old people get, our parents can still fuck us up worse than anyone. But that's on her. Not you."

"I know. And I'm proud to be who I am. I just..."

"It goes back to what we said before. You want to live. You weren't doing that, Gav. You were wrapped up in work and trying to make up for who you are. That's not a life."

Gavin gave Mason that innocent yet seductive grin. "The life I've been living these past few weeks has been pretty fun."

That was all it took for blood to rush to Mason's cock. He and Gavin have had this tit for tat thing going since they met. He knew he owed Gavin a part of himself for what Gavin just gave him, but that would have to wait. "Come here."

Gavin didn't need any prodding. He leaned toward Mason and kissed him. It was a slow kiss, an owning kind of kiss, and in this moment, Mason would gladly give himself over to the man. Let him possess him and have him any way Gavin wanted.

He just needed to be had.

But he wanted to own a little bit, too.

"Let's go." Mason stood and walked toward the hallway. Gavin was right behind him as Mason headed for Gavin's bedroom. The second they stepped inside, Mason pulled Gavin's shirt over his head. Leaning forward, he circled Gavin's nipple with his tongue.

"I want your ass."

Gavin shook his head. "I thought—"

"Not that. You'll still do the fucking, but I want to taste it. Finger it. Eat it. Drive you fucking wild before you take me. You good?" Mason always paid attention to his lifestyle and choices. Since he was a bottom, he knew his body well and kept himself as prepared as he could.

"Yeah, we're good," Gavin replied, hearing what Mason asked him.

"I like that about you." Mason covered Gavin's mouth with his. Plunged his tongue inside for a quick, demanding kiss, before ripping away. "You're good at telling me what I want to hear."

***

Mason had a way of making him want to talk about things that he usually kept to himself. He had a way of making Gavin feel like someone else, and want to do things he'd never done.

He made him feel comfortable.

And he turned him on like hell, too. No matter who did the fucking, Mason called the shots, and Gavin liked that.

He moaned when Mason's large hand shoved down the back of his jeans. As their cocks rubbed together through their denim and Mason's mouth found his neck.

"Bite it." Gavin fisted his hand in Mason's hair, pushing him closer to his throat.

He loved the hunger Mason showed, the urgency and need. It made his dick jerk in his jeans.

"I'm saving my mouth for something else." Mason winked at him and then unbuttoned and unzipped Gavin's pants. "Finish."

Gavin did as Mason said as he took off his clothes as well. The man's body about wrecked him—firm, cut muscles, but not over the top. Dark hair, and a hard cock that Gavin suddenly wanted in his mouth.

He reached for Mason's erection, but his lover shook his head and then pushed Gavin on the bed. "My mouth, your ass. Play nice."

So Gavin grabbed his own cock instead. He ran his thumb over the head, smeared the pre-come there as desire flared in Mason's eyes.

"You don't play fair."

"Would you want me to?" Gavin responded.

"Hell no. Now turn over."

Gavin's pulse beat wildly, like a drum solo, loud and eager. He wanted Mason's tongue on him, *in* him, and then he wanted to fuck the man senseless.

Rolling, he laid on his stomach, with a pillow under his arms.

"Here." Mason grabbed another pillow and shoved it beneath his hips. "I told you I'd want your ass. It's so fucking sexy." He rested between Gavin's spread legs, and ran a finger up and down his crack.

"Damn…" Gavin shivered. "Hurry."

"No."

"Then bend the hell over so I can fuck you." Gavin reached for Mason, hoping the man wouldn't call his bluff. He didn't. With a hand at the base of Gavin's back, he pushed him down, then let his fingers roam down Gavin's body. With one palm on each check, he spread them wide.

"That's what I want to see. That tight hole waiting for my tongue." And then his face was between Gavin's ass cheeks. He lapped at his asshole, over and over.

"Oh, fuck." Gavin's eyes rolled back. There was nothing, nothing like the feel of a tongue in his ass. Fire started to build beneath his skin, a small blaze that grazed the surface, as it spread.

He pushed, trying to get close to Mason. Trying to feel more of him in more places. He wanted something inside him. Wanted to be stretched, the teasing pain that came before the pleasure. "Fingers." Gavin gritted out.

"You read my mind, music man." He glanced back to see Mason suck on his own fingers, getting them nice and wet. Gavin's body thrummed with excitement. His prick burned as he rubbed it against the thick comforter.

His hands fisted in the pillow when Mason worked two fingers inside him. It had been too long since he'd been penetrated, since he felt someone inside him. Even though they'd been together numerous times, this was the first time he'd gone near Gavin's ass.

"Fuck...yes. Go faster," he begged.

Mason's fingers thrust forward, went deep and then pulled out again.

"I want my tongue on you, too."

Gavin went lightheaded when a wet tongue flicked over his hole. Mason kept it up, fingering and licking until Gavin thought he would go insane. He pumped his hips, let his dick thrust against the bed as Mason owned his hole for the first time. It wasn't with his cock, but *fuck*, this still worked him just as well.

"Stop." The word forced itself from his lips, because stopping was the last thing he wanted Mason to do. "You have to fucking stop or I'm going to lose it." And then Mason would have to get him hard again so Gavin could fuck him.

Mason didn't slow down. Didn't stop fingering his ass. Licking his hole. Gavin didn't stop thrusting, either—into the bed, then pushing his ass in Mason's face.

It was the combination of the three, the friction on his rod and the play behind, that got him.

He buried his face in the pillow. His whole body tensed in the best way, tensed in the way that said it was preparing to let go.

When Mason's fingers pushed in deeper, when they went for his prostate, rubbing the sensitive spot, Gavin couldn't hold it back. He thrust again, his cock leaking all over the bed. Mason's tongue circled him again, making him shoot again, then again, as he emptied his load.

Damned if his body didn't feel like deadweight. Like Mason has taken everything out of him. *Fuck.*

There was a rustling behind him. Mason's tongue was gone, and then his fingers, and then his weight. Gavin rolled just as Mason went up on his knees, jerking himself off.

"Christ, you got me right there. Just fucking watching you and I'm right there."

No way could Gavin not be a part of this. He wet his fingers in his mouth, then reached a hand up and behind Mason. He bent over Gavin's body, ass in the air, using one hand to hold himself up and the other to work his dick.

Gavin pushed his fingers inside. Wished like hell it was his half-hard cock inside Mason.

It didn't take long—a few hard thrusts of Gavin's fingers, a few pumps of Mason's hand, and then he erupted, ribbons of white, sticky come landing on Gavin's stomach, mixing with his own.

As Mason went down, his heavy weight astride Gavin, all he could think about was how explosive they were together.

How good they felt together, and not just when they fucked, either.

He hadn't expected it to happen….but he was damn glad it did.

Chapter Twenty-One

Gavin stirred, naked, beneath him. Mason pried his eyes open, not even aware that he'd fallen asleep. Darkness still encased the room, telling him that it was the middle of the night. Mason's body was sticky, and as he ran a hand down Gavin's abs, he realized his lover was the same.

"You weren't kidding about the small window between orgasm and passing out, were you?" Mason's hand vibrated on Gavin's chest as he spoke, his voice scratchy.

"Hey, not all the time. I'm always up for a round two, and it doesn't sound like I'm the only one who fell asleep."

"I'm sorry. About the shit with Isaac. I'm not usually a jealous man. I don't know what's wrong with me."

"You're a man. You want to know what's yours is yours. I get it. I'm not fucking my ex. I won't fuck my ex. But if we're going to do this, you have to trust me. I don't play games, and I don't take shit, either." Mason rubbed his thumb through the hair on Gavin's chest, wanted to feel it against his skin. "Don't accuse me again, and if you're in, we'll define everything right now. There's something about you that I can't get out of my head."

Had he been looking for a relationship? Hell, no, but he might have found one. Mason was okay with that. And if Gavin wanted to keep it strictly fucking, he'd deal with that, as well.

Gavin turned, threw a heavy leg over Mason. He fucking loved that. The weight of another man on top of him. Gavin's hand went down, cupped Mason's balls.

"Are you asking me to be your boyfriend?" Gavin questioned.

"We're not twelve. I'm just asking you if you want to be mine."

His body started to respond to Gavin's hand. Blood flooded is dick.

"Yeah...yeah, I think I do. Now, you owe me. Tit for tat, remember? How'd it go when you went home?"

Damn it. He'd hoped they could avoid that and Gavin would just take his ass. "We're awfully fucking chatty. Are we supposed to spend this much time talking?"

"Do people come with rule books about what they are and aren't supposed to do? We're living, right? That's what it is. Go with the flow. This was your idea, boss."

Yeah, he guessed it was. "It's nothing, really. I just...even when I wasn't living the life I wanted, I always felt like I knew who I was. Now? I'm not so sure. That's a hard pill to swallow at thirty years old. And should it even fucking matter? Who my parents are or what my heritage is? I know my personal history, and that's all that should matter. My head just keeps fucking it all up by overthinking everything. I don't fail, Gav. I never have. And not being able to get over this—that feels like a failure to me, and I'm having a hard time with it."

Pride could fuck people up more than anything else, he thought.

"You've been dealt a blow. It makes sense."

That didn't mean he had to like it. It didn't mean he was okay with how he felt. "I find myself second guessing everything. Earlier, you said you're angry. I am, too. I'm pissed they lied and pissed it matters. I'm pissed that I'm not theirs."

"You are in the ways that count."

Mason shook his head. "Just words. All those are just words. What matters is how you feel. You get that. I know you do."

There was a pause, and Mason knew Gavin realized he was right. They were both dealing with shit that stemmed from something inside them. Something personal, that made them feel or act a certain way. Something that made them human.

"Have you ever thought about finding her? Your birth mother? Might help." Gavin rolled over and lay on top of him. Mason wrapped his arms around him. That's what he wanted. Muscle on muscle. Chest on chest. Cock against cock.

"She's in Durango. I know that. And she has a husband and she's clean. Why do I need to see her?"

"Because you're not dealing well?"

Just what he wanted to hear. "See, now you're just trying to emasculate me." Mason leaned down and kissed Gavin's forehead.

"You know what I mean."

Mason sighed. "I do." And he knew why he didn't want to find her, either. She hadn't wanted him. Maybe it was the drugs at first, but once she got clean, she still hadn't wanted him. Mason didn't know why that mattered so much, but it did.

"Can we end the talk for now? Fuck me and put me to sleep."

"Whatever you say, boss."

Gavin did exactly what he said.

***

Mason boxed him in against the bar. "Hurry, get on your knees before someone comes in."

Gavin rolled his eyes at Mason. "I have something more important than a blow job going on right now."

"There are things that are more important than blow jobs?" Mason retorted.

Gavin mulled that over before he smiled. "You're right. I don't know what I was thinking. There's nothing more important that getting head, but music is a close second. I found a band who wants to play two Fridays a month. They're from Boulder but they're looking to expand. They're incredible. I told them you need to hear them first, but you'll think they're great. They have this really rich sound. If things go well—"

"Book them."

He wanted that, badly. Patrons would like them. Gavin knew it.

"We can schedule them to play for you first. Make sure it's what you're looking for."

"Just book them. You like them. I trust you. You have better taste in music than I do anyway. And I'm pissed at you, too. You said you'd teach me to play. Scared I'll give you a run for your money?" Mason went to walk away but Gavin grabbed his arm.

In a lot of ways, this was something little, but Mason's trust in him meant a lot. "I'll teach you. And thanks. For all of this. Is this one of those times where I want to kiss you?"

Mason laughed. "Now you're catching on. It is." Gavin leaned in when the door made its familiar creak. That damn door. Mason had been saying he needed to fix it from the first day Gavin started work here.

"I need to fix that," Mason said at the same time Cooper said, "I love that half the town is gay now. See what you did when you turned me?"

Mason let out a loud laugh and stepped away from Gavin.

"Of course, it's always about you," Noah teased.

Cooper reminded Gavin of Braden.

He listened as Noah, Cooper and Mason continued to razz each other. He liked the dynamic of the people he'd met in Blackcreek. It made him feel at home in a way that was totally foreign to him. "Can I get you guys anything?"

"Just lunch. Burger and fries," Noah told him, and Gavin went back to tell the cook before returning.

"Hey, what are you guys doing this weekend? Noah and I were thinking of having a poker night at the house. Braden and Wes are coming. You guys are welcome."

"It'd have to be Sunday for us. Gavin and I both work Friday and Saturday night."

"I'm sure that's workable. I'll call Wes later and make sure that's something they can do," Noah told them.

Gavin smiled, feeling almost content for the first time in his life. He'd lost his job, and things were a mess with his family, but he was happy. He had a relationship that meant a lot to him and friends he enjoyed. Even the bar; who would have thought he'd enjoy tending bar? But he did. He loved the people, and was excited for the chance to bring good music here.

Music. That's something he missed. Live bands in Creekside were one thing, but he still had an ache inside him because music wasn't as big a part of his life as it had been.

"Oh, Braden mentioned you're giving piano lessons to Jess at the fire house the other day. One of the other guys is interested for his son. He wants to play guitar. Did Braden ask you about it?" Cooper leaned on the bar.

"No...he didn't." Private lessons wasn't something he put a lot of thought into doing. Jessie was one thing since she was Braden's little girl. If he decided to take more clients on, he would have to make more plans on going about it the right way.

Mason leaned close to his ear. "Do it. You want to. I can see it."

And he did. He missed instructing. It was a part of him—teaching—more than he'd realized. Just as Gavin was about to answer, the phone rang. Something made him turn and watch Mason as he sauntered over and answered it. It took less than five seconds for the smile to fall from his face.

Gavin's stomach dropped to the floor as he made his way over to his lover.

"I'll be right there." Mason hung up the phone and looked at Gavin. "It's my dad. He had a stroke."

Chapter Twenty-Two

"I have to go." Mason patted his pocket to make sure his cell was there before he headed for his office to get his keys.

"Do they know anything? Is he okay?" Gavin walked right at his heels.

"He's alive. They're at the hospital. That's all I know." He unlocked his office with the work keys and then grabbed the others from his drawer. Christ. A stroke. He could have died. Maybe he still would. *And I've treated them like shit. He raised me and loved me and I've been a fucking child over things that didn't matter.*

Mason was already out his office door when Gavin spoke. "Maybe you shouldn't drive. Let me get my stuff. I'll take you."

"No." Mason shook his head. "The bar. I need you to take care of the bar. There's nothing you can do for me in Denver." As soon as the words left his mouth he realized how they sounded. "Shit. Not that you don't—"

"I don't need you to coddle me, Mason. I'm a big boy. I get it. Call me when you get there."

Thank you. It meant a lot to him that Gavin understood. "I will. You know how to count down the register at night and everything, right? There are numbers in my drawer if you need help. Shit. I don't even have much help for you." He'd run on barebones staff since he opened. Not because he couldn't afford it, but because the bar was *his*. It was Mason's responsibility, and he wanted to do this on his own.

"Go. I have it under control."

Mason nodded, hoping Gavin saw the appreciation on his face, and then he ran to his SUV. The tires squealed as he pulled from the parking lot and onto the street.

Mason's heart punched wildly against his chest the whole drive. Stroke. His father wasn't old—in his fifties—and yet he'd seemed under the weather the last few times Mason saw him. And now he'd had a stroke. The thought made his pulse go faster, harder.

He paid no attention to the speed limit and it still felt like it took too long to get to Denver. By the time he ran through the doors of the hospital, he saw it had been less than an hour since the call.

He turned down the wrong hallway once before finally making his way to the ER waiting room. "I'm looking for my father, Ted Alexander. He—"

"Mase."

Mason turned at the sound of Isaac's voice. His ex pulled him into a hug that made Mason's heart stop beating. "He's okay?" What if something happened on the drive over?

"Yeah, they think so. We were in his office, talking about Boulder and Durango, when he went over. I wasn't sure if it was heart attack or stroke but he's been taking aspirin daily, so I gave him one—"

Mason pulled back. "He's on an aspirin a day?" Which meant they worried about the fear of a heart attack. Which meant they'd been worried about health issues that Mason didn't know about.

"Mase..."

"Christ, Isaac. How do you know more about my family than I do? What happened? How long has he been on them?"

"Not long, and it's not a big deal. His doctor decided he needed to be on an aspirin. That's all. They didn't ask me to keep this from you. I guess they just figured since they only ordered him to take one pill a day, and to exercise, he didn't think there was a reason to bring it up. We both would have done the same thing."

But it was a big deal. The comment about his dad's treadmill and the way his mom cooked the other day made more sense now. They'd worried about his health, and Mason had been too selfish to notice what was going on. He'd been too wrapped up in a past that shouldn't matter to pay attention to the future. His bar had become more important than anything else. The pressure of the restaurants and Mason himself had to have played a role in his dad's stress level. He left his family out to dry—the people who'd wanted him. Who'd chosen him. Who'd loved him.

It wasn't a mistake he would make again.

***

Gavin checked his cell for what had to be the hundredth time today. He closed the bar a few minutes before. With his phone again not indicating any calls, he had nothing much to do except go home.

He'd called Mason once, without a reply. The silence made his gut weigh down like an anchor, but he couldn't harass the man, either. He had to be dealing with a lot. All Gavin could do is hope everything was okay.

He slept fitfully all night. Thoughts of Mason, his parents and Gavin's own blocked out much chance of him sleeping. It was an easy reminder how quickly life could change. It always took a major event to remind people of that.

Gavin had just been thinking about how good things were going—that they were looking up. They spent their days fucking, laughing and working. How much better could it get? One phone call later, he discovered Mason could have lost his father. And Gavin's own dad hadn't been healthy for a while. His mother, either, yet he hadn't as much as called her since their fight.

Gavin rolled over just as the sun teased with coming morning. He reached for his cell off his bedside table and opened a text message. **Everything okay?**

A minute later his phone rang, Mason's name on the screen. "Hey."

Mason's voice was all gravel when he responded with, "Hey."

"Is he doing okay?"

Mason sighed and Gavin imagined him rubbing a hand over his face in frustration.

"Yeah, he seems to be. He's awake. They've been worried about his heart, Gav. Told him to take aspirin and exercise and to lower stress, and the whole time I've kept my fucking distance like a goddamned child and left the business up to him and Isaac."

He heard the pain in Mason's voice. Understood it because he would feel the same, yet, "It's not your fault. You didn't know. Even if you had, some things are out of our control. You were hurt. You dealt with it the only way you knew how."

He could have sworn he heard Mason say, *I didn't deal with it at all*, but when he asked Mason to repeat it, the man only said, "Never mind."

"You didn't have any problems at the bar last night, right? We get those random busy weeknights from time to time. And the front door, it sticks sometimes, and feels like it's locked when it's not. Did you check it?"

Why was he not surprised that's where Mason's mind would go? Sex and the bar were the two things he thought about the most. "It's fine. I have it under control. You worry about your dad. I'm here. Whatever you need, I'll help." He was sincere about that. Mason meant a lot to him, and he wanted to be there for the man.

The line was quiet, nothing except his and Mason's breathing. Finally, his lover said, "Thanks. I appreciate that. Jesus, I can't believe this happened. Do you think you can open the bar today? I'll be in at some point. There…there's a few things we need to talk about."

There was a hitch to Mason's voice then. Gavin had never heard it there before.

"Yeah. It's under control. Are you sure you're okay?" he asked.

Before Mason could reply, there was another voice in the background. "Mason, you need to get some sleep. You've been awake all night."

Gavin squeezed the phone in his hand. It made sense for Isaac to be with Mason. It did. They were friends, and Isaac was close to Mason's family. But that didn't mean he liked it.

"He's right. I can hardly hold my damn eyes open over here. I'm going to crash for a while, and then go see my dad before I come home. Thanks for helping out."

Gavin nodded as though Mason could see him. "No problem."

After they said their goodbyes, Gavin sat on the edge of the bed, his right knee bouncing up and down. It made him an asshole to be jealous right now. Mason's father was in the hospital, and it wasn't like Gavin didn't have things going on in his own life as well. Isaac should be the last thing on his mind, yet all he could think about was the fact that Gavin was here, and Isaac was with Mason, where Gavin wanted to be.

Chapter Twenty-Three

It took Mason longer in Denver than he thought it would. He'd slept for almost six hours before making it back to the hospital. His mom had refused to leave, but had practically shoved him and Isaac out. She had a pullout bed in his father's room, so he'd felt okay about leaving her, and he'd obviously needed the rest.

The talk at the hospital hadn't been easy, but it needed to be done. He ignored the fact that he felt like the room closed in on him, getting smaller and smaller the longer he was there.

Mason was a selfish man. He hadn't realized that about himself until recently. He knew he had to change it.

And he would.

Finally, after another long day, he made his way back to Blackcreek. He would have been screwed without Gavin there to help the past two days. What would he have done? What would he do now? Because the fact was, he would need a lot more help in the near future.

The sun started to set as he pulled into the parking lot of the bar. There were about ten cars in the lot, which wasn't too bad. Thankfully this had all happened on a weeknight.

Adrenaline built inside him as Mason made his way to the old, creaky door. This was where he wanted to be. This place was *his*. The thing he'd chosen his family over. The place he wasn't sure he would be able to keep.

Gavin stood behind the bar, serving drinks, when Mason stepped inside. His lover didn't notice him there, and Mason took a minute to watch him. His movements were more confident. He laughed with a couple as he mixed their drinks, obviously telling a story by the way his lips kept moving and the animation in his body.

For the first time since he got the phone call about his dad, Mason found himself smiling. He didn't know what the hell it was about this man that made him feel so...*good,* but he did.

And then he thought about his dad in that hospital bed again, and his mom by dad's side. About the changes coming up and his behavior with his family, and his muscles turned to stone again. His gut cramped up and the smile dropped from his face.

At the same time, Gavin looked up and saw him there. He paused a second, watching Mason, before he jerked his head back slightly as if to say *come here.*

Mason tried to ignore everything weighing him down and made his way over to Gavin. The couple he'd been speaking with were now in their own conversation as Mason crossed his arms and tried to pretend his life wasn't changing. "Becoming a bossy bastard, aren't you?"

Gavin's posture loosened. He leaned slightly toward Mason, crossing his arms the same way Mason did. "How is he?"

Obviously he wasn't going to let Mason pretend nothing had happened. That's what they did, though, wasn't it? Neither of them let the other get away with shit. They called each other out on it and had this standing honesty between them that Mason wasn't sure he'd ever had with anyone before. "Same."

"How are you?" he asked next.

"We'll talk later." He grabbed the back of Gavin's head and pulled Gavin toward him, pressing a kiss to his forehead. "How are things here? I need to check stock and put in an order. There are a few other things I need to make sure get finished up that I missed yesterday."

He was fully aware that he hadn't let Gavin answer his first question, but that was Mason. Or it always had been. If something needed to be done, he made sure to do it. He put work first, and everything else second. It's why he and Isaac had worked so well together. He only hoped Gavin would be able to deal with it as well.

***

Gavin kept his eyes on Mason all night. There was a tenseness in his shoulders that Gavin hadn't seen there before. His smiled forced, and his gait heavy.

Which should be expected. His father had a stroke. That was enough to stress anyone out. But it didn't stop there. Gavin wasn't sure what else weighed so heavily on his lover, but he had no doubt there was something.

And he wanted to fix it.

Wanted it gone.

It was the first time he wanted something like that for another man, the first time he wanted to fix whatever was broken because Gavin felt the overwhelming need to take care of what was his. He'd never really let something be *his* before, other than his career. He felt that way about Mason.

Gavin waited until they closed the bar down. He hung out while Mason took care of orders and paperwork and whatever he could find to keep himself busy.

Finally, Gavin pushed his way into Mason's office. The man sat behind his desk; his eyes jerked up when Gavin walked in.

"Hey. I'm just about done here. If you need to go—"

"You know I don't need to go." He squeezed between Mason and the desk. Pushed his paperwork and laptop out of the way, and sat on the desk. Mason grinned up at him and Gavin shook his head. He wasn't going to let his lover do that. He wasn't going to let him distract Gavin with sex the way he had the other night.

"So, what do we do from here, boss? What's going on that I need to know about?"

Mason's right brow quirked up. "How do you know there's something you need to know about?"

Gavin shrugged. "Maybe I've spent so much time with my dick in your ass that I'm actually getting to know you? Either that or it's the talking that's doing it. Still not sure which. I'll let you know when I figure it out."

For the first time tonight, the smile on Mason's face looked real. "Funny man, all of a sudden, aren't you?"

Gavin ran his hand through Mason's hair. Gripped it and gave it a slight tug. "Tell me, Mase."

Mason sighed and then dropped his forehead onto Gavin's knee. Gavin still had a hand in his hair, only now he used his thumb to rub the back of Mason's head. One deep breath later, Mason sat up. "He could have died. He could have fucking died, and it would have happened with me being an asshole because, what? They raised me? Accepted me and gave me everything when they didn't have to?"

"No. Fuck that." Gavin wouldn't let him blame himself. Not that he didn't want Mason and his family to mend their relationship, but he wouldn't deal with Mason being angry at himself, either. "Don't trivialize your feelings. You were hurt. We all get that way. They raised you, but they lied to you as well. Loving someone doesn't mean you're perfect. They weren't, and you weren't, either. Don't use that as an excuse."

Mason studied Gavin for a long time before he nodded. "Fair enough. That doesn't change the fact that he could have died. I left a lot on their plate when I came to Blackcreek. I never told them I didn't want the business. Then one day I just said I needed a break and wanted to try and see what I could do with a bar. It wasn't fair to them. They're my family. The business is my responsibility, and Dad...he's not going to be able to keep going at the same pace he was."

Which meant Mason would have to step in. Gavin got that. It still felt like some of the security he'd built here came crashing down with Mason's statement. "The bar?" Mason loved this place. It would kill him to let it go, whether it's what he believed he needed to do or not.

Mason let out a slow, deep breath. His hands pulled into tight fists that he banged gently on the desk. "I can't let it go. I should. Fuck, it's just a bar, but it's *my* bar. I don't want to walk away from it."

"Then don't," Gavin said simply. "I walked away from my job without a fight. Don't do the same thing. You'll regret it. You deserve to have your dream, too."

Mason's hands opened. He wrapped them around Gavin and pulled himself closer, so he fit between Gavin's legs. "You're damned smart, music man. That's why I keep you around."

"That the only reason?" Gavin asked.

"Nope. Your dick, too. You're pretty good with it."

"Only pretty good?" Gavin countered, and then, "so what are you going to do?"

Mason shrugged. "Talk to Isaac. Maybe he can deal with everything if I take over Sundays and Mondays. I can work here my five days and then spend my days off in Denver. I can deal with Boulder and Denver from there; we just have to hope things straighten out in Durango without an intervention."

Gavin fought to keep his body from turning to stone. Fought not to feel that tug of jealousy that he had no right to feel. He hated that Isaac got to be Mason's answer. For once, he wanted to be someone's answer. He wanted to be Mason's.

"No days off?" Gavin asked.

"You gotta do what you gotta do. Jesus, you know it's going to kill me to leave this place for two days every week. I can hardly keep from doing drive-bys now on my days off. This is the first thing I've ever had

162

that is completely mine. It's something I'm building for me. But they're my family. I owe them."

If there was one thing Gavin understood, it was the feeling of owing your family. For him, the reasons were completely different, but his parents had always loved him. They were his family. If you didn't take care of your family, what else was there?

"We'll figure it out. I know I'm new here, but if you want to change my schedule so I'm here when you're off, we can do that. I understand if you want to hire someone with more experience, but—"

"Hey, Gavin?" Mason interrupted him.

"Yeah?"

"Thank you."

And maybe Isaac got to help Mason with his family, but Gavin had this. "You'll owe me." He winked at his lover.

"I hope so." Mason paused and then added, "Are you going to kiss me now, or do I have to tell you to do it again?"

Gavin tried to forget everything else—his family, Mason's dad's stroke, how their schedules would change and the fact that Mason would be in Denver with his ex for two days every week. Instead he did exactly what Mason told him to do, and kissed the hell out of him.

His dick hardened, and he'd do about anything to fuck Mason senseless right now, but instead he stood and nodded toward the stage, hoping this was the right thing to do.

"Where we going, music man?"

"To have your first lesson. You're tense. Music helps me. Maybe it will help you as well."

Mason gave him a simple nod and then followed Gavin to the stage, where they spent the next hour playing together.

Chapter Twenty-Four

The next couple weeks were crazy. Mason spent Tuesday thru Saturday working at Creekside. Sunday and Monday he stayed in Denver, not only to help with the restaurant, but also to help his mom with his dad. The stroke affected the left side of his body. He struggled moving it on his own, and was also in a wheelchair for now. They hoped with physical therapy he would gain control back, but there was no guarantee.

Jesus, it made his chest ache to see his father like that. To know how close he came to death. And he would have gone with Mason being angry at him. With their relationship strained.

And honestly, they were still living that way because Mason had no clue what to say to him.

His time with Gavin had been severely cut into as well. He was tired and overworked. Gavin spent a lot of time at the bar, but work time and play time were two different things.

As far as Mason knew, he still hadn't spoken to his family, and that worried him, yet he hadn't even had the time to talk to Gavin about it.

It was a Monday morning when Mason jogged down the stairs in his family home. He had meetings today about the possibly of opening of another location that he hadn't even known about before his dad had the stroke.

It was a bad idea. Probably the worst idea there was, but his father and Isaac both pushed for it, so Mason decided to listen. There was a man that owned a failing restaurant who, as far as Mason could tell, wanted to cut his losses and run. Isaac and his father wanted to buy. It was cheap, yes, but it still felt like a colossal screw-up to Mason.

Coffee. Before anything, he needed a cup of coffee, so he went for the kitchen.

"Oh, Mason. I didn't realize you were up." His mom wiped her eyes and smiled at him.

It was the first time he'd seen her cry since everything happened. He knew she needed it but would try to hide it. That's how she worked. "It's okay to be sad, you know? Or angry. That's okay as well." He poured himself a cup and then sat at the table with her.

"Why? It doesn't change anything."

He sighed. "No, I guess it doesn't. It might help, though." He was one to talk. Blood or not, he got his stubbornness from the woman sitting across from him.

"I'd rather talk about you. How are you holding up with all of this?"

Scared. Overwhelmed. Angry. "Good. I'm not sure about this new move, though. Buying another restaurant? Now just doesn't seem like it's the best time for that."

This time it was his mom's turn to sigh. "I'm afraid you're right, but I also think Isaac can handle it. He knows what he's doing. If it was the three of you, I wouldn't doubt it, but with your dad sick, and you..." She took a sip of her coffee. "You don't want to be here, Mason. I know that. Isaac and your father see it. I know things have been...difficult, but we love you. Alexander's was supposed to be yours, and I don't see why that's changed just because we're not..." She shook her head as though she couldn't finish. Guilt swung and kicked at all of Mason's internal organs.

"That's not what it is. I left before I knew." But they'd thought he planned to come back.

"Then what is it?"

Everything. How could he explain to the woman who raised him that he felt trapped? That he felt out of place here, and at Alexander's? That he'd even felt trapped with Isaac. That he woke up one morning and realized he didn't know for sure what he wanted, but it wasn't the life he led. It would only hurt her, only make her feel guilt she didn't deserve to feel. "It's nothing. Everything is fine. I should go shower. Isaac and I are meeting soon."

His mom smiled at that. "The two of you always worked so well together."

Because all they'd ever really cared about was work. "He'll always be a part of our lives. He's as in love with Alexander's as Dad is. We won't get back together, though."

"Are you sure?" She raised a brow the way Mason often did.

"You're a damn gossip." He winked at her. "It won't happen. Plus,

I'm seeing someone else." He went to stand and realized his mistake. Now the questions would come.

"Sit your ass back down, Mason Alexander. You have some explaining to do! How is it my only son is in a relationship and I don't know about it?"

Her eyes went wide, as though she wasn't sure if she should have said that, and damned if that didn't hurt. Mason wasn't sure if it was because he felt guilty she would be insecure to call him her son, or because he needed her to be confident in who he was, so he himself could be.

"It's relatively new, and I don't even know if it's serious." Which was the biggest fucking lie he'd told in a long time. He wanted it to be serious with Gavin.

"Bring him around. We'd love to meet him."

Mason leaned over and kissed her cheek. "We'll see. Things are a little hectic for both of us right now without trying to arrange family meet-ups. I need to go get in the shower before I'm late to meet Isaac."

Mason reached the kitchen door before he stopped and looked back at her. "I love you, Mom."

Her eyes welled with tears. "I love you, too, son."

***

Gavin's car idled in his mother's driveway. Mason's dad's stroke was a constant reminder that you just never knew what would happen. His parents were older. Neither of them was in the best health. It would kill him if something happened to one of them. Especially with things the way they were now.

After getting out of the car, he headed for the front door, and knocked. He'd done that since the day he moved out—knocked on his parent's door. It used to surprise him that Braden never did, though he guessed that was pretty normal. His family just had a different kind of relationship than Braden had with his.

It took his mom minutes to get to the door. He heard both locks before it slowly pulled open.

"Oh, Gavin. I'm so glad you're here. I've been praying for you. The whole church is praying that you'd be okay and that you'd find your way back home."

She pulled him into a hug and he closed his eyes, fought the urge to tell her he hadn't found his way back anywhere. She'd asked him to leave, so he had. He didn't need their prayers because there was nothing wrong with him.

"That's why you're here, isn't it? You thought about what I said. You see what your lifestyle has done, how it caused you to lose your job and threatened your family."

He couldn't hold back at that. "It's not being gay that caused those things, it's ignorance."

"That's what the devil wants you to believe, Gavin. That's how he works. He twists things around, makes you believe in what's wrong."

"No, Mom. It's not." Gavin stepped inside the house. "Let's go sit down." He closed the door and helped his mother into the kitchen and to the table. It was old; everything in the house was. His parents had never cared much about material things.

Gavin pulled out a chair for her, and once she took a seat, he grabbed one for himself. "The man I'm seeing…his father had a stroke a couple weeks ago."

"No." She shook her head. "I don't want to hear this, Gavin. Don't you get it? Your lifestyle is wrong."

"You might believe that, but it doesn't change who I am. You might not want to hear it, but that doesn't make it less true. Mason could have lost his father. I don't want to lose you and Dad. You're my parents, shouldn't that be all that matters? This is who I am. It's not changing. If we're going to have any kind of relationship, who I love can't matter."

The tears were already coming, and damned if they didn't hurt. He was thirty years old and it still pained him to make his mother cry. "It's not right. It's not love. You're being selfish. Your…" she shook her head. "*That man,* you said his father isn't doing well. Doesn't that wake you up? Your own daddy is the same, and it's more important to you to be with some man, living in sin, than to give him the comfort of believing his son will be with him again some day."

"So I'm supposed to lie about who I am?"

"You're supposed to put your family first! Live your life however you want, but care enough about us not to flaunt it here. I don't want to hear about it. Your dad, he gets upset and agitated so easily. Give him some peace, Gavin. Love your family enough to do that. Is it really that hard?"

Her words struck something deep inside of him. She was asking him to pretend. Asking him to do something that he never wanted to do again, but then, did he want to cause problems for his father? He knew enough about dementia to know how easily agitated they could become. Was it wrong of his mom to love his dad enough to want him to live peacefully? Was it really selfish of him not to agree to just…keep his mouth closed? To pretend to be the son his parents want when he's around his father?

"It's not going to change anything. I'll still be gay. You'll still have your beliefs about my life, even if they're not spoken aloud."

"Maybe—"

"It's who I am. It will never change. I don't want it to."

"You'll go to Hell, Gavin."

He didn't believe that but he knew she did. "Then I guess that's my fate."

Chapter Twenty-Five

Another week passed in the blink of an eye. It was Sunday when Mason opened the door to his parent's house.

"God damn it!" His father's words were loud, but slurred. It would take a while for him to learn to speak clearly again—if ever. Mason's head throbbed. He wanted nothing but to go upstairs and crash, but his dad didn't shout like that often—though he had more recently.

"I'm trying, here. I don't know what you want me to do!" his mom countered, and that pain in his head got worse. It traveled down to his chest. They were falling apart.

"Everything okay?" Isaac said from behind him. Christ, he'd forgotten the man was with him.

"Yeah, it's fine. I'll be right back." He avoided the stairs and went toward the room on this level that his parents moved into.

"Where's Mason?" his dad asked, prompting Mason to stop outside the room.

"He's at work with Isaac."

There was a pause, and then he heard the struggle in his father's voice to get the words right when he spoke. "He doesn't want it. I'll never be able to work again. He doesn't want Alexander's."

It was as though someone shoved a knife right below his ribcage. With each of his dad's words, the knife twisted in deeper.

"No...he doesn't. And as hard as that is, I want him to be happy. We'll be okay, sweetheart. You'll get better. Alexander's will always be ours. We're not going to lose it. Eventually it will go to Mason. He might have changed his mind by then. I just think...I think he's lost right now. He doesn't know who he is, or where he came from. Maybe—"

"NO!"

His mom sighed. "She gave birth to him. That will never change. I think he wants to know her, even if he'll never admit it. Even if it's only to get answers. He's a grown man. He has the right to make that decision if it's what he wants."

Mason leaned against the wall and closed his eyes. He loved the two people in the next room, but he did wonder where he came from. It was a natural curiosity, he thought, but it also felt like a betrayal.

The longer their silence went, the heavier it got for Mason, until he couldn't handle it anymore. Quietly, he walked down the hallway. Shook his head at Isaac, who stood in the living room, as he opened and closed the front door loudly.

"Mason?" His mom called from the room.

"Yeah, it's me." He went down the hallway and greeted them both. "How are you guys doing today? Pop, how are you?"

His dad nodded but Mason could see how much he held himself back. "Good." There was a gruffness to his one-word reply that made that knife go deeper again.

"Isaac is out there. We were going to discuss business with you, but my head is killing me tonight. I think I'm going to tell him he can go and we can talk tomorrow. Does that work?"

Both his parents agreed and Mason told them goodnight. Isaac leaned against the stairs, close enough to have heard what Mason said. His arms were crossed in his cocky, questioning way. Mason held up a hand. "Not tonight."

"What happened?" Isaac asked.

"Nothing. Everything is fine. I just have a headache."

He lowered his voice. "That why you pretended to come home after you did? And I hear orgasms help with headaches. Want me to come up with you?"

"God damn, do you ever stop?" He had enough shit going on in his life. He didn't want to deal with Isaac, too.

"Hey." Isaac grabbed his arm. "I'm giving you shit. What happened? You know I'm here to talk if you need it."

In reality, he did know that. He just couldn't find the words with Isaac. "Same old shit, just a different day. Come over in the morning and we'll figure things out, okay?"

He took the stairs two at a time, knowing Isaac would let himself out. Mason kicked out of his shoes the second he got into his room. Pants and shirt came next, and then he fell into bed. His head really was killing him. He'd had a constant pain there for damn near a week.

He glanced at the clock on the bedside table. Gavin would still be at the bar. What the hell would he have done without the man these last few weeks? He really came through for Mason. He not only did a great job in Mason's absence, but he dealt with Mason's obsessive phone calls and written instructions about a job Gavin already knew.

A smile tugged at his lips. It would serve him right if Gavin stopped answering his calls, but Mason knew he wouldn't. Gavin didn't work that way.

Mason couldn't count on him forever, though. *I'll never be able to work again.* His father's words replayed in his head.

Where did that leave them all? Isaac was loyal to the bone, but he was also damn ambitious. Soon he would want something of his own, which is why his parents had always been happy about the two of them together. They could run Alexander's the way his parents had.

"Fuck." Mason closed his eyes, hoping to make all the shit overcrowding his brain quiet down. He owed the people in this house right now. He loved them, too. It was his obligation to be the person his family needed.

***

Gavin just climbed into bed when his cell rang. He grabbed it from the bedside table to see Mason's name on the screen. "Hey. Perfect timing. I just got home from getting the bar closed up."

"Really? Took you that long, huh?"

Despite Mason's joking words, his voice held the husky tone of sleep. "Ha ha, funny man. You sound tired as hell, yet you couldn't keep yourself from calling to see how things went with your bar today, I see."

"Or I called to see how you are."

Gavin liked the sound of that probably more than he should. "Okay, so you're tired but you couldn't help but call to see how your bar is doing and talk to me." Because the bar was in there. Gavin knew that, and he couldn't fault him for it, either.

"Maybe a little." Gavin heard something else in Mason's voice this time. The exhaustion was there, but it wasn't the only thing.

"You're working too hard. You need a day off."

"Nah, I just have a headache."

"Which head?"

"Who's the funny man now?" Mason countered. "And both."

Gavin wasn't sure what made him ask, but he knew the words were important. "Something happen?" He worried about Mason—the pressure of working two jobs and driving between Blackcreek, Denver, and Boulder so much. It wasn't healthy for him.

Mason groaned. "I almost wished we hadn't started this whole talking thing. You know the rules, tit for tat, right?"

Gavin did know, even though like Mason, he'd rather not discuss it. "What if I don't have anything to talk about?"

"You do. If not, make something up so I'm not doing this all by myself."

Gavin laughed. Mason always made him do that. He'd had a long day himself and had been looking forward to crashing, but now he found he was doing exactly what he wanted to do. Talking to Mason. "Okay. You first."

"I walked in on my father yelling and cursing. It's not something he's ever done. They say a stroke can sometimes change parts of your personality. I'm hoping it's just that he had a bad day. Or maybe it's the fact that he also felt forced to admit to my mother that he knows I don't want Alexander's. He's angry and hurt, which I understand. Add in the fact that he's dealing with the realization he might never work again, and from the sound of it, arguing with my mom on whether or not they should tell me my birth mom's name. I miss my bar, and my boyfriend, and my ex won't quit trying to fuck me and it's pretty much been the day from hell."

"Well, that's where I'm going, so hopefully it's not too bad," Gavin tried to tease, but Mason practically growled into the phone in response.

"Not funny. What happened?"

"I went to see my mom last week. She reiterated where I'm going to spend eternity and asked me to pretend to be someone I'm not." Just another day.

"Shit. Last week? Why didn't you tell me?"

"Because you have enough to worry about."

Mason paused and then said, "I still want to know. Look at us, we're a couple of sob stories. Aren't we supposed to be living our lives, jumping out of planes and spending whole days in bed doing nothing except sleeping and fucking?"

"And playing music. Don't forget that."

177

"Never. You're sexy as hell when you play. And at least we're not sob stories alone."

That was true. The responsibility they both felt to their family, to do and be something for the people they loved, had always been a common bond between them.

"Let's change the subject, music man."

"Isaac is still trying to fuck you, huh?" Shit. He hadn't meant for that to come out. "Fuck, I didn't mean—"

"Are we really going to argue about my ex again? I had a shitty day, and he half teasingly offered me an orgasm. I said no, came to bed, and slept until I woke up to call you—the boyfriend I said I miss, if you didn't hear that part."

And now Gavin felt like an ass. He shook his head, almost reached for the light as though that would make a difference, but didn't. "You're right. I don't know why the hell I can't let that go. And I miss you, too."

"Good." Gavin heard a rustling sound on the other end of the line before Mason asked, "Have you gotten off today?"

Gavin liked where this was going. "No."

"Then let's do it. Take off your clothes. I'm damned good at phone sex. Dirty talk gets me hard."

Yeah, it did Gavin, as well. At least from Mason. Standing up, he pulled off his clothes the way his lover told him to.

Chapter Twenty-Six

Mason didn't want to think about everything that happened today. He didn't want to consider that he hadn't been willing to talk to his oldest friend but had easily opened up to Gavin. The only thought or feeling he welcomed right now was pleasure—to get off and get Gavin off as well.

"Are you naked?" he asked.

"Yeah. That's not really something you typically have to ask me twice to do."

He chuckled at Gavin's joke. Smiled at the huskiness that already set in Gavin's tone. He needed this just as much as Mason did.

"I know you can get off by jerking yourself off and listening to me talk to you, but I want you to picture what I'm going to be doing, too. I'll be pretending you're fucking me, Gav. I'll use a few fingers and try and make myself believe it's your cock."

"Fuck yes," Gavin hissed out.

"Hey, are you starting without me?"

Gavin countered, "Hurry up then."

Mason grabbed his lube. "Tell me what you're doing."

"I thought you were going to do the dirty talk?"

Ah, so he hit a nerve with his lover. Gavin wasn't very experienced in being a vocal lover. "Some of it. Paint me a picture. Tell me what you're doing. Are the lights on or off?"

"Off."

"Turn them on so you can see." He heard movement on the other end of the line.

"The light next to the bed is on. Damn, I am so fucking hard. There's a vein on the top, runs from base to head. I can see it pulsing beneath the skin."

Mason groaned, wishing like hell he could be there to see it as well. "Run your thumb up it. Pretend it's my tongue. I'm licking you nice and slow."

"Yeah... Want you here."

"I'm there. I bet you have a bead of pre-come at the tip just waiting for my tongue."

More movement. Mason's own erection ached like crazy. He squirted lube in his hand and rubbed his prick slowly. "Is it there?" he asked.

"Yeah...yeah, it's there."

"Rub your finger in it." He paused. "You do it?"

"Yes."

"Now put your finger in your mouth. Lick it off before you fuck your hand again."

"Holy fucking shit. You're killing me over here."

Mason laughed, moved his hand faster. "Me, too. Ask me what I'm doing, Gavin."

The sound of deep breaths filled the line before Gavin did as he was told. "What are you doing?"

"My first finger is at my hole. It's so damned needy. It wants to be filled. I'm rubbing it but it's not enough." And it wasn't. Mason held the phone between his shoulder and ear so he could use one hand to work his cock and the other to tease his asshole.

"Push it in. It's me. I'm sliding my finger into your ass. I'm going to fuck you with it."

Mason's cock jerked against his stomach. "That's what I want to hear." He pushed his finger in. "Give me another one."

"Whatever you say, boss."

"Harder, Gavin. You know how I like it. You know I want more." Mason let a second finger join the first, thrusting in and out of his hole. "My hand is still on you. Should I use my mouth? Let you fuck my throat?"

"Yes. Oh, God, it feels so fucking good."

"Use your other hand on your balls. Make 'em feel good, too." Mason curved his finger, looking for his prostate to send him over the edge. "Harder. Fuck harder," he told Gavin.

"Fuck," Gavin groaned out. "I'm coming. Damn, I shot all the way up my chest."

Mason pushed, rubbed his finger on his prostate, and watched as come pumped out of him, landing on his stomach, in his belly button, ran down his side. It was like all the pressure inside him built up and then just exploded, and it was gone. "Jesus, I needed that."

"Yeah," Mason's voice sounded scratchier than it usually did. "I did, too. Felt good."

"You feel good."

Gavin didn't respond, but Mason could hear him breathing.

"I had a shitty day, music man. Didn't really want to deal with anyone. Didn't want to talk to anyone…except you. Thought you should know that." Because it was true, and Mason would never be a liar.

"Yeah… I feel the same. It's crazy, the connection I feel. But I'm right there with you."

Mason found himself smiling. He wasn't the sappy type. Hell, he'd never really talked to a man he was with the way he did Gavin, not even Isaac. But again, he wasn't a liar, either. The one thing he didn't want to do was pretend with Gavin. They were both on this journey of living their lives, and holding any of that back wouldn't be true to it. "It's the sex. Good sex can change your life."

Gavin laughed, and Mason knew neither of them thought it was just about the sex.

"My time between orgasm and sleep is about used up. Don't clean yourself off. Sleep with your come on your body and pretend it's mine."

He was about to hang up when Gavin said, "Wait."

"Yes?"

"Thanks. For everything."

Mason felt this contentment sort of ease through him, settle into his muscles and bones. "Nothing to thank me for." And there wasn't. Somehow the two of them ended up in this together.

***

"Remember your promise to me, Gavin. A good man keeps his word. It's not good for him when he gets agitated. It takes days to recover sometimes, and—"

"Do you really think I would purposely hurt my own father?" Is that the way she saw him?

"That's not what I'm saying, but the truth is, you've hurt him before. You've hurt both of us. You've hurt yourself."

It always came back to that. And how in the hell did his sexuality affect them? It was his life, and it made the distance between them grow even more that his mom would rather he live a lie his whole life than "hurt" them by being true to himself.

"Maybe you don't see it like that. You may think you're a homosexual, but that's the devil's—"

"That's enough!" Gavin paced away from her before he said something he couldn't take back. "I know you don't understand, and I know you were raised to believe certain things, but don't tell me I don't know who I am. Don't tell me that I've hurt you both by being me."

His mom shook her head. "Gavin...I...we just worry about you so much."

He sighed, walked over and kissed her cheek. "I know, Mom. I'm going to get in there. You go get your hair done and then come back. We'll be here, and Dad will be okay. I promise."

He left his mom to go on her way. Gavin made his way to the locked ward where they kept dementia patients. He checked in at the font desk, trying to hold back that anger surging through him. "How's he doing today?" Gavin asked, probably stalling.

"It's been a pretty good day. Nothing out of the ordinary as far as confusion or outbursts. I'm sure he'll be so happy to see you."

Would he? If he was in his right mind and remembered who Gavin was, would he be happy? The knots in his gut tightened. It was a unique feeling, going to see his father in a nursing home, and not one he enjoyed. Ridiculous as it was, he always saw his dad as this invincible being. His parents were old-fashioned. His dad was always the one to *take care of the family.*

They stuck to their gender roles. If there was a problem, it was up to his dad to fix it, and now here he was, wasting away in a nursing home, and he couldn't fix it. None of them could.

"You're welcome to go in, Mr. Davis."

"Thank you," Gavin replied to the woman behind the desk. When he got to his father's room, the door was closed. He knocked softly on it before slipping it partway open. "Dad? It's Gavin."

"Who?"

Gavin's heart dropped. "Gavin." He stepped inside. "Do you remember who I am?"

An unfamiliar anger flashed in his dad's eyes. "Of course I know who you are. I'm not an idiot." He shook his head. "I apologize. I'm going crazy being locked in this room."

Gavin's eyes scanned the small, sterile-looking room. Yeah, he could get that. "Do you want to go for a walk?" His mom told him they had a garden out back where he could take his dad out to walk if he wanted.

"Could we do that?" Finally there was a familiar light in his father's eyes. They'd been so close when Gavin was young. Then, after they discovered he was gay, the pain in his dad's eyes always kept Gavin at bay. When he decided to pretend he wasn't who he really was, things were better again. That's the man who looked at him now. The one who was proud of him, and damned if Gavin didn't like that look. He wanted his parents proud of who he was regardless of who he felt attracted to.

"Absolutely. Come on." Gavin helped his dad out of the chair. He linked his right arm through his father's left one and slowly led him toward the door. After checking him out, he went for the gardens were they could walk.

"The air feels good, doesn't it?" The sun burned bright, but they were lucky to have a slight wind. Summer had always been his favorite time of year.

"It does. Reminds me of fishing with you."

Gavin's head whipped his dad's way at that. He would never get used to this—lucid moments followed by confusion. It was this constant fear every time he saw his father, not knowing what to expect. But this...the memories were something he hadn't brought up before.

"We used to have a lot of fun, didn't we?" Gavin asked.

"We did." His father squeezed his arm. "Our boy. Your mother and I always wanted you so much. We were so proud of you—being in the church band, college, your job. I..." he shook his head. "We had our hard times when we worried about you so much. It about broke your mom...those things...those thoughts you used to have." Gavin's eyes fell closed and he let out a deep breath. *Don't do this, Dad. Don't go there.*

"We prayed for you every day. The whole church did, and now we have our boy back. It's a miracle."

No, no it wasn't. He was the same Gavin, and that would never change. And it shouldn't matter. "I've always been me. It's the only person I know how to be, Dad."

And damned if it didn't make him want to go postal on the whole fucking world that his family didn't like the person that was.

Chapter Twenty-Seven

Mason smiled when Gavin walked into the bar. "Hey. What are you doing here? You're giving Jessie a piano lesson today, right?"

"We did it early this morning. She has a friend's birthday party this afternoon. She's damn good for her age. I hope she sticks with it. I'm excited to see where she can go with it. Piano is a tough instrument. I loved it, but I almost quit at one point. I think most kids go through that. It's probably my favorite to play now—that and the guitar."

Mason crossed his arms, enjoying the passion in Gavin's eyes. That was one of his favorite things about the man, how passionate he was about music, and his love for it.

"What?" Gavin asked.

"Nothing. Kiss me."

Gavin leaned over the bar and took Mason's mouth. Mason didn't let it go on as long as he wanted to, not wanting to risk someone walking in on them.

Since they didn't currently have any customers, he walked to the other side of the counter and took the stool beside Gavin. "Do you think I can disappear for a couple hours tomorrow? I'd like to go to my father's doctor appointment with him. He's gained a small amount of movement back on his left side."

"Yeah, sure. No problem."

Mason rested his elbows on the bar and leaned his head into his hands. He closed his eyes, taking a minute to rest. "Thanks. You've been a life saver, you know that?"

When Gavin didn't answer, he slid his hand up, resting his forehead in it, and turned to see his lover. The man studied him, looked at him like he wasn't really sure who Mason was. This time it was his turn to ask, "What?"

"You're exhausted and not taking care of yourself."

Mason tried to smile. "Why don't you take care of me, then?" He knew what Gavin meant but didn't really want to go there right now. He needed time off. He needed to lessen his trips to Denver, not add more.

"Stop pretending you don't know what I mean." Gavin stood, and scooted behind him. Mason groaned when Gavin's hands started to knead the muscles in his shoulders.

"You're going to make me come."

"You probably need that, too."

"I always need that." He closed his eyes and enjoyed the strong hands on his shoulders, his neck, working all the tight muscles there. "You have talented hands."

"Comes from years of playing instruments."

"Can we do this every day?" Mason pleaded.

"Hey, how is that fair to me?"

"You get to touch me? Ouch, shit." Gavin's teeth bit into Mason's shoulder. "I was going to invite you to lunch at my folks house this Sunday, but now I don't know…"

Gavin's hands paused.

"My family would like to meet you. I'm warning you that Isaac will probably be there, but if you want to come, you're welcome. We can get the bar covered for a few hours." Mason was fully aware this visit propelled their relationship forward, and he was okay with that.

"I'd like that. I'm going to show him you're mine."

He chuckled. "This possessive side of you is pretty hot, but it's not needed."

The door creaked but Mason didn't move. Gavin's hands stopped massaging but he kept them on Mason's shoulders.

"Jesus fucking Christ."

Mason recognized the angry voice behind him. He turned and kept Gavin close as a group of firemen came in. Braden and Cooper among them, though it had been the homophobic prick Fred who'd spoken.

"Problem?" Mason asked.

Fred just shook his head, but the set in his body said he did. From what Cooper and Noah had told him, the problems with Fred went back to when Cooper and Noah first got together. They only grew when Braden fell in love with Wes. They'd come to an understanding at work, after an intervention with their captain, but that didn't mean it changed the way Fred obviously felt.

"That's good." He didn't take his eyes off Fred as he spoke, letting him know Mason wouldn't deal with his shit. Not in his bar, or anywhere else.

Braden grabbed onto Fred's shoulders. It was meant to look playful, but Mason could see the anger in his eyes. "Be careful with the water here, Freddy boy. I heard it makes you gay."

Everyone laughed except Gavin, Mason, and Fred, who shoved Braden away. Mason didn't have the energy to laugh.

"Watch out. Duty calls." He stood, kissed Gavin on the forehead, and then went over to serve the firemen and the asshole that came along with them.

***

Gavin followed Mason to his parent's house on Sunday morning. This would be the first time he met the family of someone he was in a relationship with, besides Braden. Probably because Braden had been the only man he'd been with besides a casual fuck.

And they were more. He'd realized that for a while, but this cemented it.

Gavin killed the engine as his car sat in Mason's driveway. He got out as Mason walked toward him. "Your home is incredible." It was a large, brick house, with perfectly manicured lawn and flowers. They had tall pillars out front, with a covered walkway and fountain off to the side.

He never would have pegged Mason as growing up in a place like this.

"It's a bit much if you ask me. It was a good place to grow up, though. Let's go." Mason nodded toward the house and started walking. Gavin fell into step beside him. Mason held the door open and signaled for Gavin to go in first.

The inside of the house was just as beautiful as the outside, with marble tables, crown molding and incredible artwork. "Wow."

"Don't stress, music man. Just a house. I promise they're much more down-to-Earth than you'd expect."

"Who said I'm stressing?" Really, he was. This was a big step for them.

"Mason? We're in here!" a woman's voice called. Mason led Gavin through a set of double doors and into a large family room. Mason's mother sat on the couch, his father in a wheelchair, with Isaac in a chair across from him, showing the man some paperwork.

"Hello. You must be Gavin. It's so nice to meet you." The woman with a kind smile walked over and shook Gavin's hand.

"Hello, ma'am. It's nice to meet you as well."

Mason's eyebrows pulled together as if something surprised him. Gavin shrugged and smiled at Mason's mom.

"None of that. Call me Catherine. This is Mason's father, Ted. Ted, this is Gavin."

Before Gavin could reply, Mason asked, "What are you guys looking at?"

"Just restaurant things. We'll talk about it later." Isaac put the papers into his briefcase.

Ted looked up from his seat. "Good to meet you," he said, though his words were slightly slurred.

"You, too." Gavin held out his right hand so Ted could do the same.

"Gavin." Isaac nodded and Gavin did the same. He wasn't sure why, but he hadn't expected the man to be here already.

"What time did you get here?" Mason asked Isaac.

"I stayed the night, so I could help Mom with a few things. How was the bar last night, Mase?"

Gavin stiffened. It was strange, uncomfortable even, that his boyfriend's ex was so close to the family that he not only stayed here at times but that he called Gavin's mother Mom. Add to it that he couldn't read Isaac, didn't know him well enough to know if he meant his question honestly or if he tried to give Mason shit for not being here.

"Good. We were busy. Things are really taking off. It's good to see all my hard work paying off." The guarded edge to Mason's voice told Gavin that there was more behind Mason's words than he knew. Isaac didn't respond, though, and Mason turned his attention to his father. "Hey, Dad. Looking good today. Want to hang outside for a bit? I want to show Gavin the garden."

"If you'll excuse me, I'm going to take a shower," Isaac stood and left the room. Gavin really hated that man. He wanted him out of Mason's life. *Because you see how well he fits here...*

But he didn't, really. Not with the Mason that Gavin knew.

The four of them went out for a walk once Isaac went upstairs. The majority of the tension seemed to leave with him. They walked, and

Catherine would point out different trees and flowers that she liked. She told him stories about Mason when he was a kid. Of the time he decided to run away and tried to stay in the garden all night but got scared.

"Thanks for that, Mom. Just what a guy wants is for his boyfriend to hear he was afraid to sleep in a garden."

Gavin chuckled as she wrapped her arm around his shoulder. "That's okay. You were only twelve."

"Twelve!" Gavin asked, and then Mason and his mom both started to laugh.

"She's trying to make me look bad. I was seven."

"Eight," Catherine corrected.

"Play...ball..." Ted raised his right hand to point. It was the first time his father had spoken since they came out.

"What's that, Dad?"

Ted shook his head. "Broken the....win...win..." He groaned, and then let out a deep breath.

Catherine squeezed his shoulder. Gavin looked up at Mason, who gave him a sad smile, before bending forward. "You're trying to embarrass me, too, huh? He's talking about that time Isaac and I were playing ball in the field over there. I threw the baseball and it broke the window. We made up this crazy story about some other kids coming along and breaking it, which no one believed. I got grounded for two weeks, if I remember correctly."

"Not for breaking the window. That was an accident. You got in trouble for lying about it. You know we've always been big on the truth."

Even Gavin tensed when those words came out of her mouth. It was as though she tossed a blanket of tension over all of them, because Gavin knew that the way his lover saw it, they'd lied to him his whole life.

Chapter Twenty-Eight

Lunch could have gone better. Everyone spoke politely, and they kept the conversation going, but it was still awkward as hell. Mason felt it the whole time—a heavy weight bearing down on them—and he knew everyone else did as well.

"So, Gavin, Mason tells us you used to be a music teacher. Is that something you're looking into doing again?"

Mason eyed Gavin as he shrugged. "I'm not sure. I miss it sometimes, but...I guess I'm still trying to figure things out. Private lessons are an option as well. I've been approached by quite a few people in Blackcreek. It's just not something I have the time for right now."

That made Mason pause as he was eating. Gavin hadn't told him that. The last he knew was the conversation with Cooper, and he thought Gavin said yes. "Hey." It wasn't right for Gavin to miss out on something he wanted to do because he helped Mason.

Gavin shook his head and Mason let it go for now. They'd talk about it later.

After they finished eating, his mother excused herself to help his dad get ready for a nap.

"Do you need any help?" Mason asked but she shook her head.

"No. You're fine."

"We'll talk when I get up," his dad slurred. Mason had no doubt that they would. He wanted to know what Isaac and his Dad had been looking at when he came in.

"I'll be here." Mason waited until he heard the click of the bedroom door behind his parents before he eyed Isaac. "What were you guys looking at when I got here?"

Isaac glanced at Gavin as though he wasn't sure he could speak in front of him. Mason rolled his eyes. "I think Isaac has you figured out, Gavin. He knows you're a spy researching Alexander's for...who exactly, Isaac?"

"You're being an asshole. That's not what I was thinking." Isaac crossed his arms, and Mason continued to wait. He wanted a heads-up before the conversation with his father.

"Numbers, Mase. Did you know your parent's income was almost doubled when they purchased the Boulder location? It's smart to think about growing if the opportunity is there and it makes sense. We have one in our lap right now. The price is low, you've seen it yourself. Buying out the new location would be the smartest move we could make."

Mason's fist came down on the table. "Jesus Christ, Isaac, are you kidding me? Did you see my father?"

"Do you *know* your father? He bounces back from everything. He's already making great progress. He needs to work. Being productive will make him heal more quickly. Wasting away is not what he needs!"

He felt Gavin shift beside him, felt bad that he had to witness this, but Mason wanted him by his side as well. "Don't do that. Don't you fucking act like you know them better than I do."

"You're not acting like you know them at all. You know I can handle this, Mase. You know we can do it until your dad gets on his feet, and this would be more stability for them. This is helping him build the empire that he wanted for his son. You're thinking with your dick because you want to stay in Blackcreek, playing house with your boyfriend, instead of living the life you always planned."

A vein in Mason's head pulsed. An inferno raged through all his internal organs.

"That's going too far—"

Mason couldn't help but cut Gavin off. "Fuck you, Isaac. You don't know what I want. Just because things aren't going the way you want, don't try and pretend you know what's best for me. That you've ever cared about what anyone wants, other than yourself. You say I'm thinking with my dick and maybe I am, but you're thinking with your wallet instead of what's best for his physical well-being."

"He wants to work! And he has us. Don't you think landing this deal would make him feel good? He won't be the one out there putting in the work. I will. I'll take it all on if I need to. This is what he wanted when he opened Alexander's. He wanted this for *you*, but you're too busy feeling sorry for yourself because you think genetics is what makes a family! You're too busy punishing them to—"

"Hey, now." Gavin pushed to his feet but Mason was already there. He grabbed ahold of Isaac, pulled him up and shoved him against the wall.

Isaac and Mason were comparable in size, but the man didn't try and fight him off. "Finally, there's the fucking man I'm used to seeing in you. I had to piss you off for you to show it. You know I'm right, Mase. You—"

"Stop it! Stop it right now before your father hears you both!" The frantic, high-pitched cry in his mom's voice almost didn't get through to Mason. His body was wound up too tight. His brain ran in too many directions at once.

Was Isaac right? Was he trying to punish his parents because he wasn't theirs? Could he really not get past genetics?

"Come on, boss. Let him go. Don't do this here." Gavin touched his arm and when he did, Mason's hand fell from its hold on Isaac. He turned to see his mom's hand shaking as she held it in front of her mouth, crying. Jesus, what was wrong with him? He'd almost just kicked Isaac's ass in his family's dining room.

"Come on." Gavin's hands came down on his shoulders. "Take a walk with me. Let's go cool down."

Mason needed to do just that.

***

"Fuck!" Mason yelled as soon as they were a good distance away from the house. They were in the garden, out back. Mason held his palms flat against a tree, leaning on it, his forehead pressed to the bark. "Tell me I don't want to move forward with this new restaurant for the right reasons, Gav. Tell me it's not because I'm only thinking about myself or because I'm pissed at them."

Gavin didn't know how to answer that. "I think your heart is in the right place. I think you want to do what's best, and I think you're trying to do what's best. I also think the people in that house don't know you as well as they think they do. Maybe you haven't let them know you as well as you should. They see someone who wants completely different things when they look at you than what I see. Until they understand that, you're going to keep going rounds."

Gavin wrapped his arms around Mason from behind. "You're hurt, too. Sometimes we don't see clearly when we're hurt. Until you deal with it, nothing's going to change."

Damned if those words didn't ring true to Gavin, too. They grew roots, inside him, made their home because he wasn't doing anything to change his situation, either.

"Do I think it's a good idea to buy another restaurant? From what I've seen, no, but what do I really know? Maybe they need the money, and maybe it really will help your dad feel better. I do know that whether they buy one or not, you don't have to work in them. I understand your commitment to your family by trying, though."

Mason sighed. "Why the hell is dealing with family so hard?"

"Because we love them and want the best for them, and sometimes that hurts us."

Gavin leaned back to give Mason space when he turned around. He had his back to the tree now. He hooked his finger in the loop of Gavin's pants and tugged. "You're smart. I knew there was a reason I liked you so much."

"I thought it was for my cock and my music."

"That, too. You make things feel better, music man. It doesn't feel so fucked up with you around. It's not about work and money and obligations with you. It's about want."

Gavin's chest got full. His body temperature kicked up. That was probably the best compliment he'd ever been given. It turned him inside out. Reflected in his eyes. "Damned, if I don't feel the same way about you."

"Look at us, a couple of saps." He shook his head. "I need to figure out where the hell my head's at. I need to get in there and talk to my mom."

Gavin agreed with him on that one. "Yeah, I think that's a good idea." He paused and then said, "Regardless, they love you, Mason. All the people in that house do, and I don't think that love is dependent on running Alexander's or not. Even your asshole ex, who I really want to knock out. Just once. Just one hit and I think I would feel better."

Mason laughed.

"I don't think he ever thought he'd lose you, and that scares him."

"I think he likes to win, and right now he's not winning. Come on. I need to get my ass back in there."

And Gavin had a lot of things he needed to figure out himself.

Chapter Twenty-Nine

Mason watched as Gavin pulled out of the driveway to go back to Blackcreek. Once his car disappeared, he let out a deep breath and walked back into the house. His mom sat at the dining room table, with her back to the door.

"Isaac left," she whispered when he got close. "He's been in your life since you were born, Mason. I can't believe you would get physical with him."

He took the chair across from her, knowing she wouldn't understand. "It was a fight. It happens. He'd try and kick my ass if I pissed him off bad enough."

Mason saw the red rings around her eyes when they made eye contact, and he quietly cursed. He didn't want to hurt his family. She latched her hands together on top of the table and Mason noticed they still shook.

"I think you need to go see her, Mason. I think you need to know your birth mom—"

"No." He shook his head. He didn't need that. The people in this house had raised him. Why did he need someone who hadn't wanted him?

"There's something going on with you. Maybe you don't see it, but it's there."

He was an adult. Who gave birth to him shouldn't matter. "I know who my family is."

She gave him a sad smile. "There's nothing wrong with wanting to see where you came from. And if you want a relationship with her..." His mom sat up straighter, and Mason could tell it was a show. That she wanted to try and look like she believed this, even though it hurt. "You deserve this. It's only natural to wonder. We should have given you this chance earlier."

"Dad—"

"You let me handle him. I'm doing what's best for you right now."

And she always had. Both of his parents always had, so why in the hell couldn't that be enough for Mason?

"It's curiosity. Who doesn't wonder where they came from? I," she shook her head. "You met her once. Your father doesn't know."

Mason's heart raced. He wanted this. Wanted information on the woman who had given him away. "He was always worried before. He said it was because of her history with drug use, but I think he was always afraid she'd want you back. I couldn't tell her no, though."

Mason leaned forward, his elbows on the table. She'd seen him? And as long as he could remember, he'd never known his dad to fear anything. Even this stroke. Isaac was right about the fact that it wouldn't get his father down. He won. He triumphed. Yet he'd been afraid of losing Mason, the very thing Mason was letting happen.

"She came to the house. We spent the afternoon in the garden. She played with you all day. I'm not going to lie and say it didn't hurt. My instinct was to hold you to me," tears poured down her face, prompting Mason to move to the chair next to her. "You were mine. Ours. Not hers. But…it was beautiful as well. To see you talking and playing with the woman who brought you into the world."

Damned if Mason's hands didn't shake, like hers did.

"That's when she got her life together. That's when…"

She married and started a new family.

Mason's mom opened her hand. She held a small, folded piece of paper inside. "Here's her phone number and address."

Mason shook his head, the word *no* on his tongue before she even finished speaking. "You're my mother, and my dad's in the next room."

She smiled, patted his hand, and then put the paper in his palm. "You want to know where you came from. I see it every time you look at me. I also know you love us. Take the information, Mason." She kissed the top of his head and walked out of the room.

***

"How are things going with you?" Braden put his feet on the railing of the back porch. Gavin just finished giving Jessie a piano lesson, and the two of them were watching her play outside.

"Busy. And you? How's married life?"

"Fucking great. I could pretty much ask you the same thing. You and Mason seem pretty serious."

Gavin shrugged because he really didn't want to go into his relationship with Braden.

Braden laughed. "I can take a hint." He nodded toward the little girl on the swing. "You're doing a good job with Jess. You miss teaching, I can tell. Why not go back to it? Or give more private lessons?"

Gavin rubbed a hand over his face and groaned. Not because he didn't agree with Braden. He'd thought about this a lot recently. Things would be different now. He wouldn't go back to not being completely open about who he was. *Except with your family...*

Gavin shoved that truth away. "I'm not sure it's the best time. I'm still trying to navigate how to work things out with my family. Mason's got a lot going on with his dad's stroke, going back and forth to Denver, and I'm helping with the bar a lot. I can't see trying to...what? Start a business right now?"

Even to his own ears they all sounded like excuses.

"Sounds like a whole lotta reasons not to do it because of everyone else. What about doing it for yourself?" Braden grinned. "See how smart I am? Being married with a kid and now I'm all grown up."

Gavin couldn't help but laugh at his friend. He wasn't sure Braden would ever grow up, but that was part of his charm.

And he also wasn't going there with the man. "We're not together anymore. You don't have to try and figure shit out for me, remember?" He winked and stood up. "I better go. Mason texted a little while ago. He wants me to go down to the bar, so he can show me something."

Braden opened his mouth but Gavin cut him off before he could speak. "Not that kind of something. Did you just say you'd grown up?" Honestly, for all Gavin knew it really was that kind of something, which he'd damn sure enjoy. He hadn't fucked Mason in over a week.

"Where's the fun in that?" Braden stood and patted Gavin's arm. "Have a good one. I'll talk to you later. And, I'm not trying to give you shit here, or trying to figure out your life for you, but you should really give some thought into the lessons. You love it. If Mason's the kind of man who deserves you, he'll understand that."

Gavin nodded but didn't go into any detail. Mason would understand. He had no doubt in his mind about that.

He made it out to his car when his phone rang. Gavin smiled, assuming it was Mason, until he saw *Mom* on the screen. His pulse kicked up a notch. It did that when she called now. Hell, maybe it always had, only now it was for a different reason. Mason's dad's stroke put things into perspective for him. You never really knew what could happen.

Gavin hit talk. "Hello."

"Hi. I need a favor from you. We have our church banquet this afternoon. We do it every year and our pianist is sick. The music is a really important part of our celebration. It would mean a lot to me if you could fill in."

Gavin dropped his head back against the seat. It made him an asshole that he didn't want to do this, but spending the day around people he knew had prayed for his soul because of who he loved didn't sound like a good time to him.

"Please. I don't ask a lot of you. It's for a good cause. We're celebrating the Lord."

Which was something Gavin didn't have a problem with—he didn't. He only had a problem with their representation of what that entailed.

Not only that, but he had Mason waiting for him. "I have plans with Mason today." He wasn't going to keep that from her. He already kept enough of himself hidden because of her belief of what it would do to his dad.

"Oh… I see. So it's happening already? You're choosing that *man* over your family? I hardly see you, Gavin. You stopped teaching to work in a bar. What happened to my son? This isn't…we've loved you and would do anything for you, and you're throwing your life away."

Do anything except fully accept him.

"It's one day, Gavin. Please. This is important to me. With your father in the home it's… it's all I have anymore."

That's what did him in. He knew how important this was. He knew how fervently she held her beliefs close to her. She dedicated her whole life to church, his dad, and Gavin. She'd been with his dad since she was seventeen years old, and now he was in a home. Gavin could do this for her. "You're right. I'd be glad to help. What time do you need me?"

"It starts in an hour."

Which meant he would already be slightly late. "I'm on my way."

"Thank you, Gavin. You know I love you, right?"

He did. He always had. "I know. I love you, too."

He called Mason as he drove. The bar sounded fairly quiet when Mason picked up.

"Hey, it's me. I'm not going to be able to make it. My mom called. I have to head home and help her with her church banquet. The pianist got sick and I need to fill in."

"Well, hell, what about my surprise?"

Gavin thought of Mason on his knees. Or being on his knees himself. Of sweat and hard bodies and fucking. Who the hell cared if Mason was at work? Gavin wanted him. That's what he had an office for, and it had been much too long since Gavin had him. "You're getting me hard. I like the sound of that."

"Hey, you using me for sex? Who said this had anything to do with fucking?"

"No, it's not just the sex, but the sex is good, too." And that was the truth. He enjoyed doing nothing but spending time with Mason—they could be sitting around the house, working at the bar, or jumping out of planes. He felt like himself around Mason more than he did anyone else.

"It is. Hey, we're slow around here. I bet I can sneak out for a couple hours and watch you play. *That* gets me hard. It feels like a Goddamned lifetime since I've done anything except work—here or Denver. It's been all the same. I need to get out. Swing by the bar and I'll follow you."

He got what Mason was saying, but the thought of Mason dealing with his mom put a heavy weight in his gut. "You don't want to spend your time out there."

"I don't, huh? You mean you don't want me to? That's okay if that's how you feel, just don't put it off on me."

What the fuck? "I'm not putting it off on you. You can't tell me you want to go spend your afternoon at a church function with the mother of your lover, who thinks her son is going to Hell."

Mason was quiet for a second and then mumbled, "Shit." There was noise on the other end of the line before he said, "Yeah, I guess you're right. I'll catch you later. I have customers."

"Mason." He wasn't sure why he said his boyfriend's name. Wasn't even sure what to say after it.

"Don't talk and drive, music man. Didn't anyone tell you that's not safe?"

"Always so damned bossy." But he sounded like Mason, and that's all that mattered to Gavin.

Chapter Thirty

Mason hung up the phone a little louder than he needed to. He didn't know why in the hell this bothered him so much. He understood feeling loyalty to your family. Mason experienced that same thing every day, yet he'd been instantly annoyed when Gavin canceled on him.

It was the stress. It had to be. And the uncertainty of the future. And the Goddamned piece of paper that felt like it taunted him every second since the day he received it.

But the truth of it was, all that had a way of falling to the back of his mind when he was with Gavin, and Mason wanted that. He needed it. And it hadn't helped that Gavin clearly hadn't wanted Mason to go home with him. He understood how Gavin's mom was, but she also knew he was gay. Mason didn't like to feel like he had to hide.

He spent his whole day moping around the bar like a damned child, angry and frustrated with Gavin. It was a big step for Mason to take Gavin home, and he wouldn't have minded the same treatment.

"Piano, huh? Some of the bands Gavin brings in need a piano, or something?" Melody, one of their regulars, sipped her martini.

"Something like that." Mason pulled some of the empty glasses off the bar.

"He runs the place well when you're not here. You can tell he wants to do a good job for you. The two of you make a sexy couple." Melody winked at him and Mason chuckled.

"Thanks. And you're much too beautiful to sit around this place every week alone."

She finished off her glass. It was almost closing time. When she came in, she typically left right before they closed for the night.

"The company in here is so much better than the company out there. I'm actually glad it wasn't meant to be the night I tried to flirt with you. It's good to see somebody I know happy." With that, Melody set a twenty on the bar and left.

And he was that. His bar made him happy, and Gavin did, too. It was all the other shit that kept getting in the way.

Mason finished up at work before locking up. He let his other employee go, and finished up everything himself. Just as he grabbed his things to head out for the night, Mason heard a key in the lock, the familiar creak of the door, and then Gavin walked in.

"Hey, I..." His eyes landed on the piano, in the corner of the stage. Gavin stared at it so damn long Mason suddenly felt nervous. It was a foreign feeling, someone having that effect on him, but he wanted this to be something good for Gavin.

"I know you miss playing. I'm not sure if this is the best place for it. We can move it to your house if you want, but I just figured you do enough helping me around this place that—actually, fuck that. That's not the whole reason. I wanted to do something nice for you, so I did."

Still, Gavin didn't answer him.

It wasn't anything special. It was a used piano, but from the research Mason did, a nice one.

"You're falling in love with me, aren't you? Shit. I knew the piano was too much."

It was those words that finally prompted Gavin to look at him. He smiled and shook his head as he pushed the door closed behind him. "You're crazy."

"Eh. You just caught me on a weird day."

Gavin locked the door, and then made his way over to Mason. His T-shirt stretched across his chest as he moved. He stopped in front of Mason and shook his head again. "I don't know what to say."

Mason could see that in him, the confusion mixed with happiness, hiding behind the shock.

The almost shy innocence that he sometimes showed came out of hiding. Mason wasn't sure what it was about that, but it always made his dick hard and his heart race. "I guess you better think of something."

"Thank you."

Mason raised a brow. Gavin could do better than that.

"I'm sorry?"

Mason crossed his arms.

"I don't deserve you, oh great one. You're sexy, and sweet, and not only the best fuck I've ever had, but you give me things I probably don't deserve."

"Better." Mason grinned before nodding toward the piano. "Come play for me, music man." He could practically feel the anxious energy rolling off his lover.

Mason went to turn, but Gavin grabbed ahold of his arm because he could. "Really, thank you, though. I don't...no one has ever done something like this for me before."

Mason shrugged, feeling uncomfortable all of a sudden. "Then I'm glad I did it."

***

Gavin's fingers felt tight. He opened and closed his hands numerous times to try to make them relax. He had absolutely no reason to feel nervous. The piano always felt like an extension of himself. Any instrument did. He'd played for church, school, and done shows. This was his element, and yet playing for Mason, on the piano Mason *bought* for him, felt like stepping into a whole other universe.

"What do you want me to play?" Gavin managed to push the words from his mouth before sitting on the bench.

"Surprise me."

And so he did. His fingers suddenly remembered that this was what they did, that they felt at home here, as they moved across the keys. The sound was slightly off from being moved, but it didn't matter. Somehow it still sounded perfect to him.

The music flowed from him, slow and then with increasing speed. The notes filled the air, welcomed him, as did the feeling of Mason behind him.

Somehow through all of this, Mason had become like music to Gavin. A constant. Something that made him feel good, that made him feel alive.

When the song ended, he went straight into another one, not wanting the feeling to stop. *This* was his element. *This* was what he was born to do. Gavin was good at this, at creating a sound for people to fall in love with. For him to fall in love with.

And he missed it like hell.

At the end of the second song, Gavin forced himself to stop. He only made it mid-turn before Mason's mouth possessed his, hungry and demanding. It took what it wanted, and Gavin would gladly give it.

Their tongues battled, and then the weight of Mason on his lap, straddling him on the piano bench, sent a whole new set of torture through him. The kind that made him want to bend Mason over the piano and fuck him senseless.

Or maybe to make love with him.

"Jesus Christ, that was sexy as hell. We're getting a piano for your house and my house, too. I want one every place you can fuck me."

Gavin didn't laugh, couldn't, because he felt so damn much right now—gratitude, friendship, and maybe even something else. "Thank you."

"You said that already." Mason fisted a hand in Gavin's hair. "But you're welcome."

He brushed his thumb over Mason's jaw, felt the rough hair that started to grow there. Wanted to feel it on his body, between his legs and his crack. "You're making me fall in love with you." Maybe he shouldn't admit that, or hell, maybe he shouldn't even feel it, but he did. Gavin tired of not jumping out of the plane, and he wouldn't hold that back with Mason.

His lover grinned. "Because I bought you a piano?"

"Because you make me laugh. You think I'm funny, too. You're loyal and honest. You make me want to live, and when I play, you see the music."

"Then my plan succeeded." Mason stood and held his hand out for Gavin. "Take me home, music man. I'll show you that you're doing the same thing to me."

Chapter Thirty-One

"It's been a long day. I need to take a shower."

Mason closed the door behind them as they stepped into Gavin's house. Christ, how the hell did this happen? He'd been with Isaac for years and had never fallen in love with him. Yes, he had love for his oldest friend, but he hadn't been *in* love with him, yet he felt himself taking a header right over the same cliff Gavin told him he leaped from.

"I'm going to join you," Mason told his lover, already following him down the hallway.

"That's fine, but I want to fuck you in my bed."

Mason grabbed his arm as he went to turn into the bathroom. "What if I want you to take me in the shower?"

"Then I guess I'll do both."

Mason laughed. "Ah, think you can go twice in a row, huh? You must be feeling pretty fucking horny."

Gavin pulled on his earlobe. "You can't handle it?" He gave Mason this cocky, sort of grin. Oh, he could handle it, all right.

"I can take anything you want to give me. Hell, I fucking want it." Only he didn't plan on having Gavin fuck him in the shower, anyway. He had something else in mind.

Gavin pulled off his shirt, and then tossed it to the floor. Leaning into the shower, he turned on the faucets. His back was sexy, muscular and strong. Mason took advantage, kissing his way down Gavin's spine as he got the water to the correct temperature.

"Mmm, that feels good."

"I like the taste of your skin. I taste your soap and a hard day's work on your body at the same time." Mason fucking loved that. He kept going down, ran his tongue in a line at the top of Gavin's jeans, tasting the skin there as well.

Gavin tensed up. "If you don't stop, I'm not going to have a choice except to fuck you in the shower."

"No fucking. Just playing." Mason swatted Gavin's ass. "Get undressed."

As Gavin did as he said, Mason undressed as well. It was no time before they were both naked and climbing into the shower. It wasn't nearly big enough for the two of them but they'd make due. The second they were inside, Mason took Gavin's mouth. Their tongues twined together, their bodies molded against each other in the same way. Mason held Gavin's face between his hands as he ravaged the man's mouth.

Water cascaded between them as he thrust his prick against Gavin's. His lover reached down, wrapped his hands around them both as they worked their cocks together.

"That's enough." Mason pulled away even though it about killed him. "No fucking in the shower, remember? You're the one who insisted on the bed."

"I changed my mind." Gavin reached for him but Mason shook his head.

"You're teasing me."

"You like it." And the truth was, teasing Gavin meant teasing himself. He wanted to come—in Gavin's mouth, or with Gavin's cock in his mouth. Either way would work, he just needed an orgasm, but he forced himself to hold off.

Mason picked up the soap, lathered his body, and then handed it to Gavin. "We're both going to have our mouths on every inch of each other's bodies. Clean up."

Gavin took the soap from Mason with a smile. He obviously liked the idea as much as Mason did.

***

Gavin rinsed his body and then turned to Mason. He'd already finished, and he had his back to Gavin, his hands flat on the shower wall. Gavin graced the curves and dips of his muscled arms, down his back, and then back up again.

"Give me your mouth," Mason told him, and damned if his whole body didn't shutter in anticipation.

He grabbed Mason's head, tilted it to the side, and then covered Mason's mouth with his own. He worked to show Mason how hungry he was for him, how much he wanted him as he owned his mouth, while his dick rubbed up and down his crack.

And then he kissed his way down Mason's back to give the man what he really wanted. What Gavin wanted, too. Water poured over his face as he kneeled behind his lover. It was distracting. All he wanted was Mason's ass, so he reached behind him and turned it off. "They make it look so hot in porn, but it's annoying me. I just want you."

Mason groaned, and pushed his ass out, spread his legs more so Gavin could have better access. He palmed Mason's cheeks, rubbed his hand down the curve of his ass and to his thighs.

"You're killin' me, Gav."

"I'm admiring."

"Admire with your tongue."

Gavin laughed. Sex had always been just that to him—sex. And this was sex, amazing sex, and it made him feel raw, and invincible, like he ruled the fucking world because Mason wanted him this much. But it was more than the sex, too, because his heart thudded, and he wanted nothing more than to please the man in front of him—more for Mason than for himself.

And then Mason's hands reached behind himself. Gavin looked up to see his forehead against the shower wall, and then he spread his own cheeks, an open invitation for Gavin to have his hole. There was something so vulnerable about it. Maybe it shouldn't seem that way because he'd known from the first night that Mason needed ass play. He wanted it fucked and licked and fingered, but this, having him hold himself open for Gavin, made his whole body spin out of control. Made him want to claim something for the first time in his life.

His whole body thrummed with need. Gavin leaned forward and

slowly, so fucking slowly it almost killed him, he circled Mason's pucker with his tongue.

"That's it. Right like that," Mason moaned from above him.

Gavin kept it slow at first, a prelude, a gentle play of his tongue on Mason's anus. The longer he ate at him, the hungrier he became, until he licked at him with more speed, his tongue lashing harder.

He buried his face between his lover's cheeks. Let his facial hair rub the sensitive skin of Mason's crack as he worked him with his mouth.

"Fuck." Mason pushed, making his ass move closer to Gavin's face. Making it move against him.

Gavin bent farther, started with his tongue between Mason's legs, and then run it up and down his crack to his balls, that hung heavy.

"Finger. Give me a finger. Need something inside me."

Damned if he wasn't honored that Gavin got to be that person, the one to fuck him and pleasure him and to call Mason his. He was pretty sure he'd give Mason whatever he wanted.

Gavin sucked his finger before rubbing it against Mason's hole. He pushed it in, watching it disappear into Mason's anus before pulling it out again. His lover still held his own cheeks apart for Gavin, so he just watched, watched the slide of his finger. Watched the hole open up and take him, the way it would soon do for his dick.

"I want two. Give me two of them." Mason spoke with a husky, sex-induced edge to his voice that made Gavin want to come right then and there.

He pulled out, wet two fingers, and then let them invade Mason's body. Just like with his tongue, he started out slow but then quickened the pace.

"Jack yourself off. I'm going to blow all over this fucking shower and I want you there with me."

Gavin smiled and gladly used his other hand to pump his dick. Up, down, up, down he jerked his cock, and fucked Mason with his fingers.

"You are so fucking sexy down there. I could have you on your knees every day and never get tired of you down there."

His balls drew up as Mason's words hit their mark. Gavin jerked harder, found Mason's prostate and rubbed the spongy spot. He leaned forward, licking at his lover's hole as he kept fucking him with his fingers, and then Mason groaned. Jerked. His ass squeezed Gavin's fingers as he spilled all over the wall. Gavin shot, too, come sliding down his hand and mixing with the droplets of water on the shower floor.

As soon as Gavin pulled his fingers free, Mason grabbed him, pulled him to his feet, his mouth close to Gavin's ear. "You're making me feel things, too, music man. Go to bed with me. Fuck me. Play for me. Show me your music."

There was nothing Gavin wanted to do more.

Chapter Thirty-Two

Mason had no worries that he'd be able to get it up again. His cock already started to stir, wanted more, and from the looks of Gavin, he didn't have to worry about his lover, either.

They climbed out of the shower together and went straight for Gavin's bedroom. Their bodies had already started to dry, but he still saw little beads of moisture on Gavin's back and shoulders. He wanted to lick them all off.

Like he said, he planned for them to have their mouths all over each other before this night was over.

"Lie down," he told Gavin when they got to the room.

"What do you want?"

"Your cock."

Gavin went down on his back, with his legs open. With half an erection already, Mason realized he wouldn't have to work very hard to get Gavin stiff again.

That didn't mean he wouldn't pretend otherwise, though.

Mason went to the foot of the bed, kneeling, and kissed the top of Gavin's foot, his ankle, and then he started to make his way up his lover's leg.

This man tied him in knots. He was caring and giving. Loyal even to his own detriment, and made Mason want to be a better person, too.

"What happened here?" He kissed a scar on Gavin's left shin. The hair on his legs moved when Mason breathed.

"I tried skateboarding once as a kid. It didn't go well."

Mason couldn't help but laugh as he continued to kiss his way up Gavin's body.

"I see how you are. I tell you one of my childhood horror stories and you laugh at me."

"Somehow I don't think you were brokenhearted about not being the next big skateboarder." Mason skipped over Gavin's hardening prick. He licked his stomach, letting his tongue wet the hair there.

The first nipple he licked, but the second he bit, prompting Gavin to groan and thrust against him. He buried his face in one of Gavin's armpits then his neck as he sucked the skin there.

"Suck my dick." Gavin grabbed ahold of Mason's short hair and pushed his head down.

"What if I don't want to?"

"Do it anyway."

Mason cocked a brow at Gavin, who added, "Please."

"Since you asked so nicely." He took Gavin deep. The head of his cock hit the back of Mason's throat. His lips stretched wide around him as he sucked his lover off.

He went down, sucked Gavin's sac, played with his balls, which made Gavin thrust. "You like that?" Sucked the sensitive sac into his mouth again, let his tongue trail down the seam.

"Fuck…"

"Soon." He pulled off just enough to wet two fingers before he went back to blowing the long, thick cock in front of him. Mason let his hands travel under Gavin's balls until his fingers found his asshole. Mason pushed, twisted and worked his way inside.

Gavin jerked. Gripped Mason's hair tighter. And he realized that Gavin might miss the feel of something other than fingers inside him. That maybe he wasn't giving his lover what he needed.

Before he could think about it any further, Gavin pulled Mason off him, flipped them so that Gavin lay on top of him.

It wasn't often that Gavin got pushy when it came to sex, and he realized he liked it when Gavin did.

Mason pulled Gavin's head down so that his ear was close to his mouth. "I want you to fuck me. Hard." Mason spread his legs and Gavin kneeled between them.

Gavin worked quickly from there. He grabbed the lube and a condom from the bedside table. Covered himself and then spread lube on both his cock and Mason's asshole.

Mason tilted his body so Gavin had the best access to his hole while he rode Mason.

"Hard," he groaned out as Gavin worked his way inside him. Once he was in, he pulled out and then slammed forward again. There was nothing gentle or slow about it. It was the hard fucking that Mason needed for him.

He wrapped his arms around Gavin, grabbed his ass and slid one of his fingers between Gavin's cheeks. He worked his finger in dry, using it in unison with each of Gavin's thrusts.

He fucking loved the stretched, full feeling of this man pounding at him. The slap of their sweaty bodies together.

Gavin changed his angle, thrusting harder, and Mason did the same with his fingers. Using them on his lover while Gavin gave him what he needed.

"Right there. Like that. You feel so fucking good," Gavin told him, and that made Mason's cock twitch. Made it let go, ribbons of white pulsing from the tip.

He knew Gavin felt it. He saw the man stiffen above him. Saw the veins in his neck pulse as he came with a growl before collapsing on top of Mason. Just where Mason wanted him.

***

"Go get your guitar, music man."

Gavin groaned at Mason's words. Not because he didn't want to play but because he didn't want to move. It was so sexy, the feeling of their hard, sticky bodies pressed together. Lying on top of the man who had somehow come to mean so much to him.

Before Gavin could respond, Mason rolled, putting Gavin beneath him. He kissed his neck and said, "I'll do it for you," and then walked over to stand in the corner of his room. Gavin liked the guitar that he had in the living room better, but at this point, he just wanted to sit here and play with Mason.

He sat up when Mason handed him the instrument, and then his lover climbed onto the bed across from him.

Gavin's pulse kicked up in a way it never had before when it came to playing. Usually when he had an instrument in his hand, it was the only time he didn't mind eyes on him, but in this moment, the nakedness he felt had nothing to do with the fact that he didn't have clothes on. He felt like he would be showing Mason his soul, though he wasn't sure why.

"Play for me. Let me see your music, Gav. I already see you."

Damned if he didn't know Mason did see him. Probably more than anyone had. Hell, maybe it didn't make sense. Maybe it was too soon, or the fact that they both had so much going on in their lives, but all he knew was that Mason saw him, and he wanted it that way.

Gavin let his fingers pluck one of the strings. The sound came out wrong to his ears, so he twisted one of the pegs and played again. He continued, working the guitar to get the sound right for a good minute. "I'm tuning."

Mason chuckled. "Thanks for he heads up, but I can see that."

"I thought maybe you didn't know how since you never do it."

"Always trying to bust my balls, funny man. Maybe that was my ploy. Feign guitar ignorance to hook a sexy music man."

It had worked.

Gavin knew he had it right when his heart came alive at the sound of the notes. That's what music did for him. Brought him alive.

So, he kept it going. Let his fingers dance up and down the frets as he played the soft melody. It was the same song from the show. He'd been working on it since, and figured this was the right time to play it for Mason.

He glanced up and could see the recognition in his lover's green eyes. Damned if he didn't feel like he saw something else, too—respect? Awe? Passion? Maybe a mixture of all of them, but it made his pulse beat harder and his fingers more nimble. It was as though they had a mind of their own, emotions of their own, as though they thought that at this moment, he was introducing music to Mason for the first time.

His music? He didn't know.

Gavin's throat was scratchy, the urge to open his mouth and let the words fall hitting him, but he swallowed them down. He didn't sing in front of people. Hell, it wasn't something he did often at all, but only in a closed room during the times he'd be alone with his music.

The bed shifted and he looked up to see Mason move closer to him. Their legs touched as they both sat cross-legged in the middle of the comforter. He closed his eyes and felt the music vibrating around them. The heat from Mason's body. The hairs on his legs against Gavin's. The air smelled like sex, and Mason, and he realized maybe that was living, having things that meant the world to you and enjoying them.

He didn't need anything more than this.

"You bare your soul when you're playing..."

He opened his eyes at Mason's words. Looked and his lover as he continued to speak. "That's really the only time. Not even when you're talking or fucking do you open yourself up the way you do when you play." Mason shrugged. "This is the real Gavin. The person I'm seeing right now. I'm a selfish bastard because I want to be the only one to see him, but I can't do that. This is who you need to show to the world."

Gavin didn't know how to respond to that, so he didn't. He just continued to play.

Chapter Thirty-Three

"We need to talk." Isaac slammed the door and then went straight for the office. Mason didn't have much choice but to follow him. He'd come off a great few days with Gavin to get an urgent call from his ex. Those never went well, and he had no doubt this would be the same.

Since their argument, they hadn't talked at all unless it was work-related. By the hard set of Isaac's body, Mason could tell that though this had to do with Alexander's, the tension was still there.

Isaac collapsed in one of the chairs and Mason the other one. "What happened?" Mason asked, his body feeling set in cement. It wasn't as if they all didn't already have too much shit on their plates. The last thing they needed was another pile added on. Isaac didn't make a big deal out of things. He saw everything as easy, like when it came to buying a new restaurant. Timing didn't matter because he felt invincible. Regardless of what was going on, he let it roll off his shoulders because he thought he could handle anything.

One look at Isaac, and Mason knew whatever he had to say would seriously fuck things up for them all.

"We have major problems in Durango. The numbers are all wrong. We're missing a shit ton of revenue—gone, unaccounted for. Oh, and Bryce is MIA."

Mason went rigid. He knew it, fucking knew they had too much going on to pay attention the way they should. "What do you mean, MIA? How do we lose a manager?"

"He decides not to open the restaurant one day and no one has seen him since. I got a call this morning. I'd just pulled out the numbers you gave me and started to go over them. I could tell something major was wrong, and then I got a call from employees who were waiting outside the restaurant. The doors were locked and Bryce is nowhere to be found."

"Motherfucker!" Mason fisted his hands, tried to keep from hitting or breaking something. They were fucked and it was all his fault. He'd pulled Durango's monthly paperwork. He'd been the one who was supposed to go over everything, yet he put it off, before finally leaving it for Isaac. Between Creekside and here, he just hadn't made it the priority he should have.

"Shit!" This time he didn't have the strength to hold himself back. Mason pushed to his feet. With one sweep of his hands, he shoved everything from the desk to the floor. Missing money was big. His parents had never had a problem like this before. *He'd* been the one to hire Bryce, and now the man had stolen from them.

He'd failed. He thought he could handle it all and he couldn't. He let himself down. He let his family down. "I'll go. I'll fix it."

"Mason." The emotion in Isaac's voice surprised him. The man was cutthroat. If someone fucked up, he had no problem telling them. Mason had fucked up.

"This was on me. I was so pissed at you guys for wanting this new restaurant and so busy trying to keep things going at the bar that I let the Durango worries go. I didn't pay attention and I need to fix it." He'd known for a while someone needed to make the trip to Durango, yet he'd put it off, figured everything was fine because he knew it would fall on him, or he'd be left with Denver and Boulder.

Isaac sighed. "How are you supposed to do that? You have your bar and shit going on here. I'll handle it."

Mason fell back into the chair again. He set his elbows on the table, his head bowed, and his hands latched behind his head. After exhaling a deep breath, he asked, "Does Dad know yet?" That's what hurt. He'd failed his father. The man who built Alexander's from nothing. The man who wanted nothing more than the son who didn't even have his own blood to have his legacy.

"No. I wanted to talk to you first. You know as well as I do he's not going to take this well."

Durango was his baby. He'd worked all hours of the day there when Mason was an infant. He grew Alexander's from the ground up from that establishment, for his family.

"I'll talk to him. And I'll go. Everything else can wait. I'm going to fix this." Mason stood. "I need to go to Blackcreek. I have to talk with Gavin, and then I'll be back. Don't talk to Dad without me." Without another word, he walked out.

***

Gavin knocked on Braden's door. His friend had called him over a little while before. Apparently he had something he wanted to run past Gavin, which knowing Braden, could mean just about anything.

When his friend didn't answer, he knocked again. Finally, the knob twisted and Braden pulled the door open. "Hey, man. How are things going?" Braden stood aside for Gavin to walk in.

"Good. How about you?" When Braden closed the door, Gavin followed him to their kitchen table and sat down.

"Keeping busy. Jess is playing with her cousins today and Wes is at work. I don't really know what to do with myself."

Gavin chuckled, not sure when he'd ever seen the man so grounded. Actually, that wasn't true. He'd never seen it before Braden met Wes.

"Do you want a beer?" Braden asked.

"Nah. I'm good." The fact that his friend continued to stall didn't escape his attention. "Spit it out, Braden. What's going on?"

"I hear the skepticism in your voice. I called you here for a good thing. Don't start stressing out on me."

It was then that Gavin realized his body was tense. He fought to relax, which pretty much became impossible when he realized something else about himself. He always assumed the worst. He'd automatically expected the worst when he got here.

"I'm not stressing out."

Braden didn't respond to that. "Listen, I had a conversation sort of fall into my lap. I was speaking with one of Jessie's friend's moms. She works for the school district, and she was telling me about this new music program they've been planning to start at the beginning of the new school year. It wouldn't be at only one school. You'd spend certain days at the elementary school, middle school and high school, but it's supposed to be a really great program. They didn't have music before because of budget cuts, so now they're starting over."

Gavin got a pain in his chest thinking about the fact that they hadn't had music. It was always one of the first things to go. Didn't people realize how important music was?

"The woman who they'd hired unfortunately had a family member need her help. She's moving out of state, which means now they have the position open. I talked to her about you, told her your experience and everything, and she said that you should apply. They're having a hard time finding someone in the area with experience. It'd be a great opportunity for you to get back to teaching, and would give you the chance to stay local." Braden leaned back. "If you get your ass in gear, I can pretty much promise you'll get the job."

Gavin scratched the lobe of his right ear. Teaching. It's what he'd always done. What he loved…he thought. No, that wasn't true, he knew he loved it. It had been his own mistakes that messed it up for him before, because he'd let it become the only thing he allowed himself to love—music and teaching, and nothing else.

Still, he thought about everything that he'd given his previous job. How he'd dedicated his life to it, and how easily he'd been asked to leave, and all because he helped a kid who was just like himself.

For the first time in his life, Gavin was living his life for himself. He wanted to hold onto that. Plus, what about Mason? He needed Gavin right now. Gavin hadn't had a whole lot of people in his life who were there for him no matter what, and he'd be damned if he wasn't that person for Mason.

"I don't know if now's the right time. I need to get my Colorado license, which I guess I could work on regardless. We don't know how things are going to go for Mason. He's running back and forth between Blackcreek and Denver, and he's counting on me to help here when he's gone. I'm not sure if he'll still need my help at the bar by the time I applied for everything necessary for me to start the job." If he even got it.

Braden stalled for a moment, and then shook his head. "You've gotta be fucking kidding me."

Gavin's defenses reared up. "What is that supposed to mean? Are you telling me that you wouldn't be there for Wes if he needed you?"

"No, I'm telling you that Wes would never let me sacrifice myself for him, the same way I wouldn't do with Wes. If that's what Mason expects—"

"Fuck you, Braden. That's not the way it is."

"You love teaching, man."

Did he? He thought so. He missed it. But he was also happier right now than he'd ever been. "How do you know that? I'm happy."

"You're a bartender—"

"Hey now—"

"That's not what I meant." Braden shook his head. "What I'm saying is that you've always taught. You've loved music for your whole life, and right now you're working as a bartender. There is nothing wrong with that if it's what you want. Is it really what you want, Gav?"

What he wanted was to be happy. What he wanted was to be there for the man he loved.

"This is the perfect opportunity for you. Don't say no. Put some thought into it. Talk to Mason, apply for everything you need to apply for. Don't just say no because you're scared."

Gavin shook his head at that. "I have nothing to be scared of."

"Are you sure about that?" Braden asked.

Yeah, yeah he was. *Am I?* "Thank you. No matter what, I appreciate you looking out for me. I just can't make any promises right now. Not when I don't know how often my parents might need me, and not when things are so up in the air for Mason." Mason needed him. He wasn't sure anyone ever needed him like that before.

They said their goodbyes and Gavin jumped in his car and drove home. The whole time his brain wouldn't shut down, thinking about Braden's offer and his accusations.

He wasn't scared. He couldn't be. He was being responsible, thinking about the people in his life that mattered. It was the honorable thing to do.

He took a quick shower, and had just pulled his white boxer briefs on when he heard the front door. The only person who should be walking into his house right now would be Mason, but Mason should be in Denver.

He stuck his head out of the door to see his lover coming down the hallway.

"What are you doing here?" Gavin asked.

"I need a reason now?" he said teasingly, but Gavin heard the tension in his voice.

"Is everything okay?"

Mason kissed his forehead. "It will be. Just work stuff, which I'll talk to you about in a second. I rushed out without a shower this morning, and I really need to get cleaned up, clear my head for a second, and then I'll be out."

The muscles in Gavin's body seized up. Mason could pretend all he wanted, but something was wrong. He could feel it.

Chapter Thirty-Four

Showers were one of the best ways to clear your head. Orgasms were the first, so Mason decided today called for both. He finished his shower with the purpose of letting Gavin fuck his brains out, and then he would sit down and talk to his lover. There had to be a reasonable explanation. He trusted Gavin's opinion, and he knew Gavin would do whatever he could to help. It's the kind of man he was. The kind Mason wanted to be, and part of the reason Mason loved him so damn much.

He pulled on a pair of underwear. The soft sound of his phone vibrating in his jeans grabbed his attention, so Mason pulled it from the pocket.

Braden.

It wasn't often the man called him, and he wasn't sure why he would be now. He almost ignored it, but something made him hit answer. "Hello."

"Hey, man. How's it going?"

Shitty. "Alright, and you?"

"Good. Listen, I'm about to overstep my bounds, and I want you to know that I get that. Tell me to shut the fuck up. I'm used to it. But knowing that I should keep my mouth shut has never made me do it in the past, and I don't plan on starting now. If you're the kind of man I think you are, you'll be damn glad I spoke up."

Mason leaned against the counter, feeling a tightness in his chest. "What's going on with Gavin?"

What else could it be?

"He has a job opportunity, running a music program through the school district. It's not a guarantee. He needs to get his licensing and a few other things taken care of ASAP, but I wanted you to know about it. Like I said, tell me to shut the fuck up and mind my own business. I probably deserve it, but whether you know it or not, you were there for me when shit hit the fan with Wes, so I thought I would return the favor. I think he needs to do this but I don't think he will. Not if he doesn't know you're on board. He's thinking about his parents and the bar and, fuck, no offense man, but he needs to be thinking about himself. I just don't want to see him pass something up and regret it later. That shit will eat a hole through your relationship faster than anything else."

Mason closed his eyes. Shook his head. Motherfucker. Braden was right. Gavin missed teaching. He was sure of that. But even if Gavin didn't, it was a decision he needed to make for himself—not because of Mason or his parents or anything else.

From the day he hired Gavin, he knew the man wouldn't be working with him forever. It wasn't where his heart lay. The closer they'd gotten, he let himself forget that. Forget it because he liked having Gavin around. Forget it because he needed Gavin in more ways than just their relationship.

"Fuck," Mason groaned. "Thanks for telling me. I'll take care of it," and then he hung up the phone.

Gavin had walked away from his job and regretted it. He hadn't fought for it. He'd accepted the loss just like he'd accepted the loss of any real kind of life, using his family and his job as an excuse. Mason wouldn't be an excuse for him. He wouldn't be the reason Gavin let life pass him by. From the beginning that hadn't been what they were about, yet he planned on asking Gavin to take over his bar so he could go to Durango for who knew how long? It could be months.

And Gavin would have done it. Would have done it because that's the kind of guy he was, giving. Would have done it because Mason was now to him the same as his job had been before. He still wasn't living for Gavin. He lived for Mason, for his parents, letting his own desires fall to the wayside.

And Mason would have let him because that's who he'd always been as well. Selfish. Because he wanted it all; in a way, like Isaac. He wanted his bar to flourish, and to fix the shit with his family and their business. It was time to realize that he couldn't do it all. Sometimes a man had to make sacrifices for those he loved. He wouldn't hold Gavin back.

***

Mason walked into the bedroom in nothing except his underwear, just as Gavin put his guitar away. Gavin watched as he paced the room for a minute before sitting on the edge of the bed.

Gavin waited for him to speak, seeing that his lover had something to say. It took a minute, but then he said, "We need to talk."

Crossing his arms, Gavin leaned against the wall. "I can tell." Anger suddenly teased him. He wasn't totally sure why he was mad, but he had a feeling he wouldn't like what Mason was about to say.

Mason looked up at him from where he sat on the bed. His features were hard, his eyes detached. The look made Gavin's gut roll.

"We have a major problem in Durango. Money is missing and a manager MIA. We've been having problems there for a while but I kept ignoring it, hoping it would get better. That obviously isn't the case. I need to go there for a few months to clean up and get things back on level ground. I'm going to close Creekside while I'm gone. I—"

"Fuck that." Gavin shoved off the wall. "You have no reason to close the bar. Why are you really doing it? Let me guess, you know about the job and you're trying to make my decisions for me? Fuck you for that, Mason. I'm an adult. I can handle my own shit. Even if I did want to take the job, that wouldn't stop me from working at the bar now. Don't be like everyone else in my life. Don't think you know who I am or what I want better than I do." Damn Mason for that. He'd never treated Gavin that way before. Gavin's family told him he wasn't gay, and Braden had always thought he'd known what was best for Gavin. And maybe when they were younger, he had, but not anymore.

Mason shoved to his feet. "But would you? Would you take that job if I'm still gone when it started and I needed you? Christ, I love that about you. You give one hundred percent of yourself to people you care about, but I'm not going to be the one to hold you back. Plus," Mason went back down to the bed.

"We both have so much shit going on, Gav. I'm torn between my family loyalty, business, and fucked in the head over my parents. You're the same way about yours and your career. Don't get me wrong. I want you. I feel you, right fucking here." He touched his chest. "But our relationship so far is based on feeling screwed up because of other people. It's based on you being there for me at the bar, and me being the one to push you when you need it. That's shit we need to be doing on our own. I don't want to be what teaching at that school was to you. I don't give a shit if you take that job or not, as long as whatever you do is what you want. Right now you're living your life dependent on what I need or what your family needs. You just replaced me with your old job. Don't you see that? You're still not living for yourself, music man. I'm using you to forget about all the shit going on in my head. I don't want that for us."

Every one of Mason's words slammed into him, rained down on him in punch after punch, hitting every one of his internal organs.

Mason was right. As much as he hated it, Mason was right.

"I love you, ya know?" And he did. He knew that. Despite all the other shit, he knew that. He felt Mason in a way he'd never felt anyone else.

"I know. I love you, too. I've fucked up too much in my life, though, and I don't want to do that with you. If we don't get our own shit figured out on our own, it's always going to weigh us down. It'll just fuck us up later. I can't be your excuse for not knowing what you want for your life, or for not going for it. I can't let you be my distraction, either. Maybe I really do want the restaurants. Maybe that's why I'd originally planned on going back. Maybe not. Maybe Mom is right and I need to sort things out with my birth mother. I just know I can't give you everything you deserve right now, no matter how much I want to."

Could Gavin say he gave Mason everything he deserved as well? He didn't know.

His feet felt like they were made of lead as Gavin walked over to his lover. He stopped in front of him, stood between Mason's legs. His arms went around the man, and Mason's did the same to him. He slid his hands down the back of Gavin's underwear, rested his head against Gavin's chest.

The tension in the room suffocated him. Somehow, even though they were walking away, it didn't feel like running. It felt like fighting— for themselves and each other.

Chapter Thirty-Five

Mason worked every day straight for the next three weeks. The accounting was a disaster, as was the restaurant itself. He still wasn't sure he'd found all the discrepancies, and he had their accountant scouring the books now, too.

They'd lost two employees, which meant being short-staffed and trying to hire new people on top of everything else.

In a lot of ways, it was a rush—the feeling of building this place up again. It was almost the way he felt when he'd bought Creekside. His dad wasn't able to be here, and Isaac kept busy with Denver and Boulder.

The responsibility of Durango fell completely on his shoulders, and as stressful as that was, Mason realized something about himself: he loved that feeling as well.

He wasn't sure what to do with that. All he knew was he felt like he was accomplishing something here. He worked to bring his father's favorite restaurant back to its former glory, which it deserved. And he was honoring his father at the same time.

He still carried the piece of paper with him that his mother had given him. A name and address in his wallet. He needed to see her as well, but one thing at a time. Alexander's deserved his attention right now, and that's what Mason gave everything to.

The same way his father had.

***

Gavin sat in the room with his dad while he slept. His mom was busy at her church today, and Gavin had felt the urge to visit with his father. It still wasn't something he did as much as he should. It hurt to look at him. To know that he was slowly losing himself and that he would probably die not remembering who Gavin was—and if he did, being disappointed in that person.

He wasn't an idiot. Even if his father remembered one day, that didn't mean he would the next, but damn he wanted to talk to him. To tell his father who he was, and for him to at least once be okay with who that person was.

"Gavin?" His voice sounded harsh; not angry, but dry and almost like a hack.

Thank you, he wanted to say. Today, his father remembered his name. "Yes, it's me, Dad. Here, let me get your some water."

He filled a cup for his father and then set it in his shaky hand. He struggled slightly to keep from spilling the drink, but Gavin held off. No man wanted to need help taking a drink of water.

"What are you doing here today?" He handed Gavin the cup.

"Coming to see you."

"Good. That's good. I miss you. I don't see you enough…I don't think."

The pain in his dad's voice made his chest hurt. He couldn't imagine losing his mind that way, those moments when he realized what was happening to him.

"I know. I need to get out here more. I'm sorry about that."

"It's okay. I'm sure you're busy with work and everything."

He could easily lie. Today, his father obviously didn't realize it was summer. Gavin couldn't do that. Not this time. "Not at the moment. I'm between jobs right now. I am getting my Colorado license, though. There's a possibility I might have a new job at the beginning of the year, if I want it. I still haven't decided."

His father's forehead wrinkled. "Why wouldn't you want it?" And then, "You like it, don't you? Teaching. You were always so good. We knew you would be, but…do you like it? I've always wondered that but I never let myself ask."

Because he'd feared the answer, and maybe because he needed that to feel proud of Gavin. The knowledge hurt, but there was nothing he could do about that.

"I do. I miss it. There's something special about introducing music to children. I just… I let it rule my life before. I guess I don't want that to happen again."

His dad laughed, then went into a coughing fit before saying, "Then don't let it."

He hadn't expected those words at all. "It's not that easy."

"It's not?" At first he sounded confused, but then Gavin realized he wasn't. "I'm losing my mind, son. Some days I don't know who you are or who my wife is. Hell, sometimes I don't know who I am. When I do, the rest of it seems pretty simple."

Gavin caught his father's eyes, trying to see the knowledge there. If there was more to what he just said, or if Gavin just wanted there to be. His first instinct was to wait, to feel him out and see what he said. The last thing he wanted was to hurt his family. For his father to get agitated because of something Gavin said. But damn, he wanted this moment. This moment between them to be honest and binding. Who knew how many more they might have.

"I guess you're right. It doesn't always feel that way, though. My boyfriend and I broke up a few weeks back. It made sense at the time, but when you say that, say that things should be easy, it makes me wonder if maybe we didn't give up too soon."

His dad was so quiet for so long, Gavin wasn't sure he would answer. When he did his voice shook. His eyes were wet. "Is it that same boy?"

Braden. He meant Braden.

"No, Dad. We ended things years ago." Gavin couldn't breathe, the air trapped in his chest as he waited.

"Do you love him? The other man?"

That was an easy question. Gavin nodded. "I do."

"I always loved your mother. So much it hurt."

Slowly, Gavin reached over and grabbed his father's hand. "I know,

Dad."

"It was never a thought, never a conscious decision I made to love her. It just happened." He paused, then added, "Was it like that for you?"

Gavin's chest felt like it expanded. Like it fucking grew, because this was the first time that anyone acknowledged that fact, that whatever he felt for another man could be love. "Yes."

The tears were rolling down his face now. It was the first time in his life that he'd ever seen his father cry. Damned if it didn't cause a lump to form in Gavin's throat.

"Everything…like I said, everything else feels so much easier right now. I couldn't see that when I was healthy. I don't know what it means for you to be gay, son. I've always believed one thing, and it hurts to fear for you, that I won't be reunited with you one day, but I can say, knowing that I'm losing who I am…did we do that to you? Try to take away who you are?"

They had, but in this moment, it all wiped away. "It doesn't matter."

Gavin stood, leaned over the bed and hugged his father while the man cried. "I'm sorry. I'm so sorry," he whispered, over and over. Maybe he would change his mind. Maybe he would forget this conversation tomorrow. But Gavin chose not to focus on that. He was taking this moment, and this would be the one he held on to. Nothing else mattered. This is who Gavin was and would always be. He was proud of that. And right now, he thought maybe his father was, as well.

Chapter Thirty-Six

Mason stared at the woman sitting across from him. Her eyes were the same shape as his. The same shade of green. Damned if he didn't have her smile, too. "I didn't come here because I want you to be my mother. I have one."

She nodded. "I know that. I would never expect anything different. I'm glad you're here, though."

They'd spoken for an hour. Not about anything of importance. The restaurant, and how she went back to school recently. They made sure to skip over the hard parts, but they couldn't do that forever. Hell, Mason didn't want to.

"They loved me. They treated me well."

"I knew they would. That's all I ever wanted for you."

Then why couldn't you do it? But then, did he want that? He fought an internal war with himself. He wished she'd wanted him enough to get clean for him, to be his mother, but he also didn't want to change the parents he had. The ones who had always loved him, and who would do anything for him.

"I'm sure that's hard for you to understand. Or maybe it's not. Maybe at this point it's too late, but I want you to know, I love you. I always have. I...I wasn't in the place where I could be the mother you deserved. They were able to give you things I never would have been able to. That's a selfish answer in a lot of ways. I should have made myself be the person you deserved, but I didn't, and there's no going back. It was never you, though. It was all my fault. Always. And I have always loved you, Mason."

Christ, it was almost as though those words lifted the weight off his chest. The question in his head that hadn't stopped in the months since he found out.

"I went to see you once. Did your mom tell you that? I wanted you back. She didn't know that, of course, but I wanted you, and then... God, you were happy. Such a smart, well-adjusted, happy kid, and she loved you with all her heart. She loved you the way I did, only she had the courage to be the mother you deserved, when I didn't. I knew I could never fight for you. You were where you belonged, and I missed out in this beautiful, smart, sweet little boy. I will always regret that."

It's incredible how much a person needs to feel wanted. Mason didn't like that about himself, that need, that he'd desired to hear those words from her, but it was true. "Thank you...thank you for doing what was best for me."

She didn't cry, and he didn't, either. *Did he get that from her?* He wondered. The fact that he could feel but he still never cried.

"Can I ask questions about you? Your life? Are you married, or do you have children?"

"No, not married. I have someone I care about, though. He's in Blackcreek. Things are…complicated at the moment, though."

His mom—no, he couldn't call her that—Cherise laughed. "Oh, I recognize the sound of that. Why do things get complicated so easily?"

Mason shrugged. "It was probably my fault. I wanted to do the right thing. I think I did. I'm still not sure, though."

"I think that's part of life. We never really know if the decisions we're making are right or wrong. If we're making them for the right reasons or not. There's only so much you can do. Trust yourself, follow your heart and your gut, and hope for the best. There's nothing more any of us can do than that."

He sure as hell hoped so, because despite the fact that he actually enjoyed what he was doing here in Durango, there was one thing he missed, one person he was still sure about. Gavin. The man was his, and Mason wanted him back.

Still, he couldn't walk away from his responsibility here.

***

"I want to buy the house. I'll understand if you don't want to sell. I can look

around for something else, but—"

"Yes." Wes grinned.

"Hey!" Braden crossed his arms. "Who said you can sell my house, Wesley?"

Wes rolled his eyes. "Will you stop giving Gavin shit? You and I both know we've talked about selling it. We both know it makes you happy that Gavin will be the one to live in it, because then, for the rest of his life, you can claim responsibility for bringing him to Blackcreek."

Wes knew his husband well. "Should I leave you two alone?" Gavin teased.

"No. We can wait until you leave. As long as it's within five minutes. But yeah, my husband is right." Braden looked at Wes. "Don't get used to it, you're not right often enough for that."

Gavin took a step backward. "You're getting yourself in trouble, Braden. He looks like he wants to kill you."

Braden winked. "It's more fun that way."

Yeah, definitely time to go. "I'll leave you two to it. We'll talk more, but I really appreciate it, man."

"I'll be back." Braden kissed Wes and then followed Gavin to the door. "Have you and Mason talked?" It had been six weeks since he left, and they hadn't spoken a word to each other.

"No, but I could call him just as easily. I'm working on me right now." For once.

"Good for you. It's good to see you happy. You deserve it. You played the part well before, but you were never really happy, were you? Not even when we were together."

"No." He knew his answer wouldn't hurt his friend's feelings. He hadn't been happy. Not totally. In certain aspects of his life, yes, but he deserved the whole package, didn't he? Everyone did.

"Wow…" Braden crossed his arms.

"What?"

"I think that's the first time I haven't made someone happy."

"You're fucking crazy." He shook his head at his friend, who laughed. "Go inside and see your husband. I have some things to take care of."

"I think you're underestimating my shock right now."

"Good bye, Braden."

Gavin jogged to his car and left.

Chapter Thirty-Seven

Mason loved Fall in Colorado. It was his favorite time of the year—the leaves changing, knowing that the snow would soon come, saying goodbye to summer. It always felt like the beginning of something, and hell, maybe that's what it was.

After knocking on the door, he pushed his hands into his pockets. Maybe it made him an asshole that he came here without calling first. It would serve him right if another man answered the door, and then he'd likely commit murder and end up in prison.

So yes, he definitely should have called first—or at least asked around.

But he hadn't. He was back in Blackcreek, and there was one place he wanted to be more than anywhere else.

The door pulled open and Gavin stood there. Christ, he was even sexier than Mason remembered. And he was wearing… "Slacks and a button-up? You look like a teacher."

Gavin scratched his earlobe. "I *am* a teacher."

That made Mason smile. Good. He was glad about that. Gavin deserved to have the career he loved so much. "A teacher who could have possibly had another man answer the door right now?"

"Is that really one of the first things you're going to say to me?"

"You have to admit, it's an important one."

Gavin sighed, held the door open, and Mason walked in. The house was decorated completely different than it had been when he left. He had no doubt the navy blue furniture and records on the walls were Gavin's things. Braden's old furniture was gone.

His eyes caught something in the corner of the room and he smiled. "You kept it."

"Free piano. Why wouldn't I?" Gavin closed the door. "And there's not another man, but I'm a teacher who everyone knows might have a man in his life."

So he hadn't been playing things the way he had been before. He wasn't living two lives. Knowing that filled Mason with warmth. "Good, on both accounts. I was afraid I'd have to hurt someone when I got here. I'm not really sure how well I'd do in prison, so I guess I better count my blessings."

"You're ignoring the fact that my partner could have been the one to take you out. He would be strong, my backup. You wouldn't want to fuck with him."

Mason got a pain in his chest. He knew he had no right to ask this question, but that wouldn't stop him. "Was there one? A backup?"

"We broke up, Mase. Do you really think you have the right to ask me that?"

Fuck. No, he didn't. Mason sat in the chair, closed his eyes and took a deep breath. "I think I want to kill him."

Gavin sighed. "I didn't fuck anyone while you were gone. I've been busy. Damn, my hand's getting tired, though."

That's what he'd needed to hear. Right or wrong, he needed to hear it. The thought of Gavin with someone else ate him up inside. "Yeah, mine, too. It's not the same, though." Especially for Mason. "Nothing was the same without you. It's funny…we weren't together very long. I've lived a whole hell of a lot more life without you than with you, but it still wasn't the same." Gavin sat on the couch across from him and didn't reply. He'd obviously gotten off work not long before. He looked tired, but still didn't take his eyes off Mason.

"I've spent the last few months in Durango, like I said. I met my birth family." He crossed his arms and watched Gavin as intensely as the man watched him. "They're good people. They're still not my real family. Those are the people who raised me. But we'll have a relationship. I'm glad for that."

He waited for a response that never came. He could see the anger in Gavin, and knew the man deserved to have it. "The restaurant there is on solid ground. We got someone good in there, we think. It took a while, but we got everything settled for Alexander's." The longer he spoke the tenser he became. Christ, he may lose him. He told Gavin they needed to figure out what they wanted for their lives, and now he had to face the knowledge that what Gavin wanted might not be him.

That wasn't the truth for Mason, though. He knew exactly who he wanted, and it was the man eying him right now.

***

We. Every time Mason spoke about the restaurant, he said *we*. It made Gavin's hands ball into fists. His chest got heavy. It pissed him off. "You don't want it, Mason. I don't care what you say to me, I know that. I understand feeling an obligation, but you're still fucking pretending. If you came here to tell me you're going back to Denver, don't bother. And I'll be the one going to prison if you're getting back with Isaac. You're—
"

"Why are we talking about Isaac?"

Gavin was on his feet in a second. In three quick strides he made his way to Mason. "Because I'm not walking away from you!" He'd walked away from too much in his life. He wouldn't walk away from Mason. "We needed this time, I agree. We had too much shit in our heads. But I walked away from my job before. I've walked away from too many things in my life, and I really will be damned before I walk away from you! I'm not going to lose you to him, to Alexander's, or anything else."

Gavin didn't have enough time to move before Mason shoved to his feet. Before Mason slammed into him, making Gavin hit the wall. Something fell down but he didn't care. All he knew was Mason's hard body pressed against his. Mason's lips crushed Gavin's as their tongues dueled.

The buttons on his shirt went flying when Mason ripped it open. They parted long enough for Gavin to pull Mason's shirt off before they were kissing again.

He wanted him. His prick ached and he wanted to fuck. Fuck hard.

He wanted to make love, slow and passionately. He wanted to do it all, but, "No."

Gavin put a hand on Mason's chest and pushed him away. "We aren't doing that. We can't answer this with sex." He wanted the words back as soon as he said them. Why was he turning down sex? They'd been combustible together, always had this passionate chemistry from the first time they met.

"Tell me I'm enough for you. I know I am. I wasn't enough for anyone else in my life, but I know I'm enough for you, Mason. You can't pretend I wasn't." There was neediness in his voice but he didn't care. He needed this. He needed this man.

"Hey." Mason dropped his forehead to Gavin's. "You're more than enough for me. That's why I'm here. It's you. I never loved Isaac the way I love you. Hell, we never even said the words to each other. I'll say them to you every fucking day if you want me to."

Gavin grabbed ahold of Mason's sides. They breathed each other's air. Held each other. And damn, it felt good. Felt right.

"What about Alexander's? We'll figure it out—if you have to go back."

Mason shook his head. "It's taken care of. Isaac is hiring someone to help him there. I know it's strange, but...my biological mom? She's the one working Durango, with her husband. In some ways Alexander's will always be mine. It's my legacy, but I spoke with my family, told them what I want and what I don't. Not just bullshitted them, but the real deal. Maybe Isaac will own it all one day, maybe he won't, but Creekside is mine. I'm not going to say it didn't feel good, fixing things in

Durango. It's how I felt with Creekside. But I belong here. Hell, maybe I'll open another bar…"

"You're a workaholic and you're going to kill me."

Gavin went to pull away but Mason stopped him. "Hey, I have never had to pretend with you. Even from the beginning, you knew who I was. I showed that person to you before I did anyone else. You're more than I deserve. I want you."

His cock started to fill with blood again, but it wasn't the only part of his body working overtime. Mason was his. He felt him in each beat of his heart. "You're back for good, then?"

Mason nodded. "I am. You said you're not walking away from me, but I'm the one who isn't walking away from you. You're stuck with me now."

Gavin would take that. "I want you in my bed every night. Move in with me. With my job at the school and your hours at the bar, it's going to be hard to work it any other way."

Mason pushed his body into Gavin's. Rubbed their cocks together through their jeans. "That depends…will you play the guitar for me every day? And the piano, too? I want you to fuck me on it as well. Christ, you and that Goddamned music gets me hard every time."

"I think I can handle that."

"That's what I want to hear. I love you, music man. You know that, right? You. Love the wonder I see when I look in your eyes. Love the way you want to do right by people. Love that you'll jump out of a plane with me like it's nothing. You're the only one I want to fly with. Tell me you know that."

"Yeah, I do. You helped me decide who I am, Mase. You saw me in a way no one ever had."

Mason held him tighter and Gavin nodded toward the piano. "Can we get started now? The playing and the making love?"

Mason gave him a cocky grin. "Now's gonna be when you want to kiss me, music man."

Gladly, Gavin did exactly what Mason said.

EPILOGUE

Mason turned the chair around backward and sat down. The lights were low in Creekside and the place was pretty packed. Noah and Cooper sat beside him, Wes and Braden next to them. On the other side sat his parents and then Isaac. There were a few teachers from the high school here as well. Gavin had made quite a few friends since he started teaching.

When Gavin walked onto the small stage, Mason couldn't help but grin. Christ, he loved the man, and he couldn't be more proud of him than he was right now.

In the grand scheme of things, playing in Mason's bar was nothing—but not to Mason, and definitely not to Gavin. It filled his chest to capacity to see his man on the stage in his bar. To know that he would sing and play the guitar, sharing such an intimate piece of himself with the world. Music lived inside Gavin, and tonight, people would see that the way Mason did every time he watched him.

"This is embarrassing. Damn, there's a lot of people out there. Did you tell the whole town?" Gavin looked at Mason, who just shrugged his shoulders, waiting for his lover to start.

Gavin sat on a stool, pulled a guitar to his lap, and then cleared his throat. He played a few covers, which everyone ate up. Mason's mom leaned over and whispered into Mason's ear how good Gavin was between each song.

And he was. He had this sexy, raspy voice that drove Mason wild. It wasn't often that Gavin sang, but every time he did, Mason fell in love with him all over again.

"I'm going to sing something a little different for you guys next. It's just something I've been playing around with. Hell, I don't even know if it's any good or not, but here it is."

Mason sat up at that. Gavin hadn't told him he'd written a song to sing. He watched intensely as Gavin's fingers began plucking at the strings. As soon as Gavin started to sing, Mason's breath caught in his throat.

Never thought of lookin' for forever
Didn't think it's somethin' I would find
Thought I was happy livin' my life
But I wasn't livin', was I? No, I wasn't livin', was I?

Never realized I spent my life drifting
Didn't have anything that was really mine
Lived my life with blinders on
Lonely, so alone, ignorin' all the signs

Nothin' was real before you

Goin' through the motions, living behind a façade
I got good at pretendin' 'til you broke down all my walls
It couldn't be anyone but you
No one else had the power to see the man inside
Not even me, no not even me. Believed my own lies
Nothin' was real before you.
The only place I never had to pretend.

You taught me how to fly, how to live
I see it in your eyes, feel it in your hold
I know I did the same for you
Gave you a place to be you. Made you mine

Lovin' someone doesn't mean your perfect
We've fucked up, started again
All I know is it's you I want
Want to be your music man

Nothin' was real before you
Goin' through the motions, living behind a façade
I got good at pretendin' until you broke down all my walls
It couldn't be anyone but you
No one else had the power to see the man inside.
Not even me, no not even me. Believed my own lies.
Nothin' was real before you. The only place I never had to pretend.

Mason's heart thumped harder than it ever had. He felt full, complete. Yes, it's something he'd experienced since he and Gavin finally made things concrete between them, but this was different. This was more.

Gavin had given Mason his music. He'd put himself out there for Mason. He hadn't thought it possible, but somehow he loved Gavin more.

***

Gavin watched as Mason practically stormed onto the stage. His damned hands were shaking like crazy, yet when Mason got to him, he forgot about it.

"You like that? I wrote it myself," he teased, as Mason pulled him to his chest.

"That was…"

Mason didn't finish, but Gavin didn't need him to. He'd known exactly what it would do to his lover when he'd written it. Mason didn't have to use words for Gavin to know how he felt. "I know."

"Good, because that's something else I'm going to need you to do for me all the time. Maybe not every day, but every week. What do you think about that?"

Gavin laughed and shook his head. "Keep dreaming."

"Don't need to. Already have everything I need."

"Come on. Your parents are down there looking at us like they want to talk."

He'd spent quite a bit of time lately getting to know Mason's family. They were great people, and they treated Gavin like one of the family. Things were still a struggle with his own mom. She loved Gavin. He knew that. And she knew about the conversation Gavin had with his father, but she still had a hard time coming to terms with it all.

Gavin didn't lie about who he was, though. Not to her or anyone else, and she realized that. She'd even gone to lunch with him and Mason once.

Mason and Gavin walked over and started talking with everyone. Mason scheduled extra help in the bar tonight, freeing him up to spend time with Gavin and his family. All of this just because they'd known Gavin would play in the bar tonight. It humbled him that they cared that much.

"Do you have a moment?" Gavin looked over to see Isaac standing beside them. Things were still slightly awkward between them. He knew Mason had had a conversation with Isaac, basically putting him into his place where Gavin was concerned. It hadn't been necessary. Gavin appreciated it, but he also trusted his partner. He knew who Mason wanted.

"Yeah. Sure."

Gavin headed for Mason's office with Isaac on his heels. Isaac and Mason's father had hired someone else to help out with the Denver and Boulder locations. It seemed to be going well. Mason consulted with them at times, but that's as far as he went into working for Alexander's.

Gavin unlocked the office door and then closed it behind them.

"I owe you an apology."

Gavin crossed his arms. He hadn't been expecting that.

"I'm sure you know Mason and I had a discussion about our past and his relationship with you."

"I do."

"I wanted to make sure you know I understand that. It was…difficult at first. I've always had Mason, and I made myself believe I always would."

"He cares about your friendship." Mason did, and Gavin understood that. They had a lot of history, and Isaac was practically a member of Mason's family.

"Yes. He does. Not that I deserve it." Isaac smiled, and Gavin found himself doing the same. "I see him…the way he is with you. What he has with you. We never had that. I'm okay with it, now. I'm sure he's told you I don't like to lose."

"Yeah, I caught onto that." Gavin chuckled.

"He's got it bad for you. I wanted to make sure you know that I see that, and that I'm happy for you both."

He knew it took a lot for Isaac to say that. He doubted they would ever be close, but he appreciated the sentiment. "Thank you." Gavin held out his hand and Isaac shook it.

When he opened the office door, Mason stood there, leaning against the wall, with his arms crossed. He raised a brow and Isaac said, "Simmer down. I'm only apologizing."

Gavin saw the surprise in Mason's eyes, but he just nodded at Isaac, who went on his way.

"That was a surprise." Mason pulled Gavin close.

"It was. Unneeded, though. I know you're mine."

"Yes, I am. And you're mine, too, music man."

Sometimes he still couldn't believe his life. How much things had changed. He'd spent his life not really knowing who he was. Or trying to keep that person under wraps. Gavin didn't have to do that anymore. He would never have to pretend again. All he'd had to do was make that decision for himself. It's all most of us have to do. It's just not always an easy road to get to the place you're comfortable doing that.

"You're forgetting something," Gavin told him.

Mason paused a second. Gavin could tell the second he caught on, because he got that grin Gavin loved so much.

"Now's gonna be when you want to kiss me."

The End

OTHER BOOKS BY RILEY HART

Blackreek series:

COLLIDE

STAY

Broken Pieces series:

BROKEN PIECES

FULL CIRCLE

Coming soon:

BEN

About the Author:

Riley Hart is the girl who wears her heart on her sleeve. She's a hopeless romantic. A lover of sexy stories, passionate men, and writing about all the trouble they can get into together. If she's not writing, you'll probably find her reading.

Riley lives in California with her awesome family, who she is thankful for everyday.

You can find her online at:

Twitter

@RileyHart5

Facebook

https://www.facebook.com/riley.hart.1238?fref=ts

Blog

www.rileyhartwrites.blogspot.com

Made in the USA
Lexington, KY
07 September 2015